9/07
N08

0/09

D1013152

Five Pages a Day: *A Writer's Journey*

Five Pages a Day: *A Writer's Journey*

Peg Kehret

Albert Whitman & Company

Morton Grove, Illinois

Library of Congress Cataloging-in-Publication Data
Kehret, Peg.
Five pages a day: a writer's journey / Peg Kehret.
p. cm.

Summary: *A biography of the author of numerous books for young people,
describing her childhood bout with polio, how she became a writer,
family relationships, and the importance of writing in her life.*

ISBN 0-8075-8650-1

1. Kehret, Peg—Juvenile literature.
2. Authors, American—20th century—Biography—Juvenile literature.
3. Children's stories—Authorship—Juvenile literature.
[1. Kehret, Peg. 2. Authors, American. 3. Women—Biography.] I. Title.
PS3561.E3748 Z464 2002 813'.54—dc21 [B] 2002016768

For information about Albert Whitman & Company,
please visit our web site at www.albertwhitman.com

Cover photo, bottom: © Todd Gipstein/CORBIS.

The quotation on p. 113 is from *Night of Fear* by Peg Kehret,
copyright © 1994 by Peg Kehret. Used by permission of Cobblehill
Books, an affiliate of Dutton Children's Books, an imprint of Penguin
Putnam Books for Young Readers, a division of Penguin Putnam Inc.

For Carl

Table of Contents

Acknowledgments

Because this book covers the whole of my writing career, I want to recognize some of the people who have assisted me along the way.

I've been fortunate to work with a few special editors who saw promise in my manuscripts and helped me mold them until they were the best that I could make them. For their dedication to excellence, my thanks to Rosanne Lauer, Abby Levine, Pat MacDonald, Kathy Tucker, and Arthur L. Zapel.

After two false starts, I found the right agent for me. Emilie Jacobson, senior vice-president of Curtis Brown, Ltd., has negotiated the contracts for thirty (and counting) of my books. She's done it with efficient good humor and has always given me sound business advice. I hope to meet her someday.

No writer walks alone. For various kinds of help and encouragement, I thank Caity Anast, Joan Arth, Dave Barbor, Barbara Brett, Donna Brooks, Joe Ann Daly, Grace Greene, Sherry Grindeland, Carolyn Haney, Mary Harris, Chauni Haslett, Susan Hawk, Magda Hitzroth, Julie Hovis, Mimi Kayden, Kathy Kinasewitz, Ilise Levine, Stephanie Owens Lurie,

Susan Myers, Annette Nall, Sharyn November, Roger Page, James Panowski, Phil Sadler, Denise Shanahan, Peggy Sharp, Meredith Mundy Wassinger, and Sharon Wuest.

I also thank the Author's Guild and the Society of Children's Book Writers and Illustrators for their advice, legal assistance, and idealism.

I've tried to be accurate and honest in this book, but some of the memories go back a long way and details could not be confirmed by other people. Any errors are mine alone.

{ I }

The *Dog Newspaper*

I began my writing career at the age of ten when I wrote and sold the *Dog Newspaper.* This weekly publication, which cost five cents a copy, reported on the local dogs.

I interviewed every neighbor who had a dog. "What exciting thing has your dog done?" I asked.

People responded, "All Fluffy does is eat, sleep, and bark at the mailman." Or, "Max's only excitement is his daily walk on the leash." Such answers did not lead to important news stories.

I didn't give up. "If your dog could talk," I asked, "what do you think he would say?"

"Feed me," was the most common answer, followed by, "Let's play."

What could a writer do with such boring material? The solution sat at my feet, wagging his tail.

The first issue of the *Dog Newspaper* featured my dog, B.J., on the entire front page. Although his life at that time was as uneventful as the lives of the other neighborhood dogs, B.J. had a unique background.

Uncle Bill, my mother's younger brother, was a soldier in the U.S. Army during World War II. While in Germany, his unit went into a town that had recently been bombed. As they searched for survivors in a destroyed building, they came across a mother dog and her litter of puppies. The mother dog was dead. So were all the puppies except one.

The soldiers, who had seen far too much of death and destruction, carefully lifted that little brown dog from his littermates. One soldier tucked the puppy inside his jacket to keep him warm. The men fed him from their own food supplies, shared water from their canteens, and decided to keep him as the company mascot.

From then on, wherever Uncle Bill and his

comrades went, the dog went, too. They named him B.J. because he was a Big Job to take care of, especially when they were fighting a war.

B.J. grew bigger and stronger as he traveled with the soldiers, tagging along on every mission and somehow surviving even when the men were too busy to pay attention to him.

As the soldiers fought to protect the free world, B.J. did his duty, too. He slept with them in foxholes; he trudged long miles across burned and barren land; he helped search rubble for signs of life. Most of all, he offered love and laughter to a group of lonely, weary men who were far from home.

When the war ended, the soldiers rejoiced. Soon they would be going home to their loved ones. But what about B.J.? They knew they could not leave him in Germany. The German people were faced with the task of rebuilding their cities and their lives; no one wanted to bother with a dog, especially a dog who belonged to the Americans.

The men decided to chip in enough money to fly B.J. back to the United States. Then they had a drawing to see who got to keep him. Each soldier wrote his name on a slip of paper and put the paper in a helmet. The winning name was drawn: Bill Showers! My uncle.

Uncle Bill lived with my family, so B.J. was flown from Germany to Minneapolis, where my parents picked him up at the airport and drove him to our home in Austin, Minnesota.

I was nine years old and delighted by the addition of this wire-haired schnauzer (at least, we thought he might be a schnauzer) to our household.

According to Uncle Bill, B.J. understood many commands in both English and German. Since none of us spoke German, we had no way to prove this claim.

B.J. quickly became my dog. Although B.J. was overjoyed when my uncle arrived home after his discharge, Uncle Bill did not stay in Austin long. He got married and headed to the University of Minnesota, where dogs were not allowed in student housing. B.J. stayed with my family.

I showered him with loving attention. I brushed him, tied ribbons on his collar, took him for walks, and read aloud to him. B.J. seemed especially fond of the Raggedy Ann and Andy stories, which were favorites of mine as well.

B.J. had lived with us for a year when I launched the *Dog Newspaper.* He was a fascinating front-page subject, and the first edition of the *Dog Newspaper* sold twelve copies.

Even though my lead story required little research, this sixty cents was not easy money. All those interviews about the neighbor dogs took time. Also, I grew up before there were copy machines, so I couldn't just go to the local copy center and run off twelve copies of the paper. Using a pencil, I wrote every word twelve times. Then I delivered my newspapers and collected my pay.

B.J. and I became famous on our block. Neighbors were enthralled by the story, and I gobbled up congratulations on my writing the way B.J. ate his dinner. All of my customers agreed to purchase the next issue of the *Dog Newspaper.*

Giddy with success, I immediately began writing the second issue. The neighborhood dogs were still every bit as boring as they had been a week earlier, so I decided to repeat my winning formula and use B.J. as the main article again. Since I had already told the only unusual thing about my dog, this time I wrote a story called "B.J.'s Gingerbread House."

Our new washing machine had arrived in a large cardboard box. I kept the box to create a special house for B.J., who slept in the basement every night.

I spent hours decorating the box, copying a picture of a gingerbread house that was in one of my books. I colored curlicues; I blistered my hands cutting designs in the cardboard; I painted flowers on the sides. The gingerbread house was absolutely breathtaking.

At bedtime that night, I took B.J. down to the basement and put his blanket in the beautiful gingerbread house. I petted him and kissed him and told him I knew he would sleep well.

The next morning, I couldn't believe my eyes. B.J. had licked the glue from the cardboard, creating a sticky mess in his beard, and had chewed the house into dozens of pieces. He pranced toward me through the wreckage that littered the floor.

This story was quite a bit shorter than the story of B.J.'s rescue from a bombed-out house in Germany—and far less interesting. I filled the rest of issue number two of the *Dog Newspaper* with stirring reports such as "Rusty Knocks over Garbage Can" and "Cleo Chases Cat." After I delivered my papers, I eagerly waited for more compliments on my exciting journalism. None came. The next issue was even worse. Since B.J. still had done nothing newsworthy, I used the front page to describe what a beautiful and great dog he was. The other dogs, as always, got brief mention on the back page. Desperate to fill the space, I even wrote a story titled "Skippy Gets a Bath."

Issue number three was a publishing disaster. Few people read it, and the only person who purchased issue number four was my grandpa. Less than one month after its launch, the *Dog Newspaper* went out of business.

I believed my writing career was over. My mistake, I thought then, was always putting my own dog on the front page. Now I realize that having dull material was an even bigger error. Would the *Dog Newspaper* have succeeded if I had featured Rusty or Fluffy or Cleo? Probably not, because Rusty, Fluffy, Cleo, and all the other neighborhood dogs hadn't done anything special.

If Fluffy had gotten lost and been returned home in a police car, or if Cleo had won a prize in a dog show, or if Rusty had given birth to puppies, then perhaps the neighbors would have wanted to read my articles.

Now I know that if I want people to read what I write, I must write something that they find interesting. I need exciting plots, unique information, and fresh insights.

When I wrote the *Dog Newspaper,* I was so caught up in the fun of creating a newspaper and getting paid for my work that I lost sight of my audience. What was in it for them? Except for the first issue, not much.

B.J. took one more plane ride, from Minneapolis to Fresno, California, where my parents moved shortly after I got married. He loved the California sunshine and spent his old age sleeping on the patio. He lived to be sixteen, a good long life for an orphaned puppy who entered the world during a wartime bombing.

No one bothered to save any issues of the *Dog Newspaper.* I can't imagine why.

{ 2 }

Polio

When I was growing up, one childhood disease was feared above all others: polio. There was not yet a polio vaccine, and polio epidemics swept through the country each year, killing hundreds of people and leaving thousands more paralyzed forever. Although some adults got polio, the disease struck mostly children.

Little was known about how polio was spread. Since epidemics usually occurred during the spring and summer, parents often kept their children away from crowded places such as swimming pools or movie theaters during warm weather in the hope that they would avoid contact with the disease. Children were warned not to drink from public water fountains. Some parents didn't allow their children to play in parks or playgrounds. Each time a new case was diagnosed, the panic increased. Fear of polio spread even faster than the disease itself.

My parents insisted that I wash my hands thoroughly before eating, made sure I got enough sleep, and encouraged me to ride my bike. Despite these good habits, I got polio when I was twelve years old.

I don't know how I got it. I hadn't met anyone who had polio. There wasn't an epidemic in Austin that year and I hadn't been anywhere else, yet one day in September, my legs buckled while I was at school. When I went home for lunch, my hands shook so much the milk sloshed over the edge of the glass. I felt sick and weak. Alarmed, Mother sent me to bed and called our doctor. The next day, tests showed I had polio.

Austin was a town of thirty thousand, not far from the Iowa border. The hospital wasn't equipped to treat polio cases so my parents took me to the Sheltering Arms, a hospital for polio patients in Minneapolis.

Because polio was so contagious, I was immediately put in an isolation ward. Not even my parents were allowed in the room with me. To protect themselves, the doctors and nurses wore gowns, masks, and gloves.

Groggy from a high fever, I soon fell asleep. When I woke up, I was paralyzed from the neck down. Terrified, I called for the nurse. She came, but could do nothing to help me.

The strict no-visitors rule deprived me of what I needed most: the comfort of my parents. The worst part of those first days of my illness was not the pain or the paralysis. It was the misery of being all alone.

Any serious misfortune can leave a victim wondering, Why me? Why was I paralyzed while my friends continued their ordinary lives? At the time I was too sick to wonder. Later I decided there is no answer. Everyone has good and bad luck at times; things happen that we can't control. By chance I was exposed to the polio virus, and by chance I had a severe case. There was no "reason" that I got sick, no one to blame, nothing to point a finger at.

The old saying that bad news comes in threes was true in my case. The original diagnosis of paralytic, or spinal, polio was followed by the news that I also had respiratory polio, which makes it hard to breathe, *and* bulbar polio, which impairs the ability to talk or swallow. Having one kind of polio was bad enough; having three kinds was overwhelming.

On the third day, still burning with fever, I was transferred to University Hospital in Minneapolis. My breathing was so shallow that the doctors feared I would need to go into an iron lung, a machine that would help me breathe. The Sheltering Arms couldn't care for patients as sick as I was.

At University Hospital, nurses draped an oxygen tent over my head and shoulders. This thick sheet of plastic, held up by a frame, was three feet above me, with the sides hanging down to touch my bed. Oxygen was released inside the "tent." The room looked foggy through the plastic, but the oxygen eased my breathing.

I ached all over, my throat hurt, and except for turning my head from side to side on the pillow, I couldn't move at all. Severe muscle cramps knotted my leg and arm muscles, but I couldn't shift position to ease the pain. When I wanted to roll from my back to my side, a nurse had to help me. If my nose ran, someone had to wipe it for me. When I itched, I couldn't scratch. I was trapped in my own body.

My parents, dressed in hospital gowns and wearing masks and gloves, came to my bedside. I realized they were allowed in because the doctors were afraid I would die.

From the moment I found out I had polio, a fear of death had lurked in the shadows of my mind. Twelve-year-olds aren't supposed to die, I thought, yet I knew it could happen. I saw the same fear in my parents' eyes and wondered if my life was nearly over.

Mother and Dad were forbidden to touch me and could stay for only a few minutes each time, but I felt safer knowing they were there.

They held a straw to my lips and coaxed me to drink. They offered food, too, but the fever had taken away my appetite. My throat hurt, it was hard to swallow, and I was flat on my back. Even in good health, it's difficult for a person to eat or drink lying down.

After eight days, my fever broke. Soon after that the oxygen tent was removed. I was going to live.

Although the life-or-death crisis was over, I was still paralyzed, and so the long process of rehabilitation began. There was no cure for polio, but the doctors thought the Sister Kenny treatments, named for the Australian nurse who first used them, might minimize the lasting effects.

The Sister Kenny treatments consisted of hot packs and muscle stretching. I had both each day. Woolen cloths were dipped in tubs of steaming water, wrung out, then draped on my bare back, arms, and legs. The first time I had the hot-packs treatment, I was sure the nurse had made a mistake and over-heated the water.

"My skin is burning!" I cried. "The water is too hot!"

"It has to be this hot to help you," the nurse said.

I soon learned that after the first searing moments, the hot packs felt good because the moist heat made my cramped muscles relax. When the cloths cooled, they were removed and fresh hot packs applied. Each time, I closed my eyes, dreading the first few moments when another steaming cloth hit my bare skin.

Physical therapy followed the hot packs. The frequent muscle spasms I'd had during the acute stage of polio had tightened my muscles, and they needed to be gradually stretched back to normal before they could regain strength.

The stretching hurt, and I dreaded my twice-daily sessions with the physical therapist. She had no patience with my tears, and I dubbed her "Mrs. Crab."

My parents returned to Austin. Dad needed to go back to work, and now that it was clear that I would live, visiting hours were again enforced.

A kind intern, Dr. Bevis, listened to my silly "knock, knock" jokes, gave colorful reports of the University of Minnesota football games, and encouraged me to work hard at my exercises. "I want to see you walk again," he said. I promised him I would try.

My eight-year-old roommate, Tommy, was in an iron lung. This tube-shaped machine enclosed all of him except his head. Bellows pumped air in and out of his lungs, causing them to expand and contract.

Tommy and I listened to the "Lone Ranger" radio programs. As we cheered for our hero, the soft "swooshing" sound of Tommy's iron lung provided an odd accompaniment to the "Lone Ranger's" stirring music.

At night, I missed my parents and worried about my future. How could I ever lead a normal life?

One morning, after three weeks of paralysis, I lay in bed rehearsing a new joke to tell Dr. Bevis. By then I had a full-blown crush on him, and my daily jokes were a way to get him to spend more time in my room.

As I waited for his visit, my leg itched. I scratched the itch, then realized what I had done. I scratched again, to be sure I really could do it. The fingers on my left hand moved back and forth.

"I can move my hand!" I yelled.

The nurses came running, followed by Dr. Bevis. Triumphantly, I demonstrated my new skill.

"Can she really do it?" Tommy asked.

"Yes," said the nurse.

"Hooray!" yelled Tommy.

Dr. Bevis beamed.

No Olympic athlete ever felt more exultant at winning a medal than I did over moving the fingers on one hand.

Slowly, I regained the use of my muscles. First my fingers moved, then my arms. Next I could sit up, and then I was able to feed myself.

A month later, I was transferred back to the Sheltering Arms where I was placed in a room with four girls my age. A common enemy creates strong bonds, and Dorothy, Alice, Shirley, and Renée soon became my best friends. They knew what it was like to battle polio; my friends back home did not.

Visitors were allowed on Wednesday evenings and Sunday afternoons. The one hundred miles between my home in Austin and the hospital in Minneapolis made Wednesdays out of the question, but my parents came every Sunday, regardless of the weather or road conditions.

I was the only girl in the room who got visitors. Dorothy's farm family couldn't leave their chores long enough to drive several hours each way; Renée's parents and Shirley's also lived too far away to come.

And then there was Alice. She had been at the Sheltering Arms for ten years. She had gotten polio before Sister Kenny developed her treatments, and as a result she had shriveled arms and legs as well as the condition known as "dropfoot," which prevented her from standing. When Alice's parents learned that she was permanently disabled, they realized they couldn't care for her and the rest of their children, too, so at the age of three Alice had become a ward of the state. She pretended not to mind, but when I heard Alice's story, I knew there were worse things than being paralyzed.

My parents soon included my roommates in their visits. Dad took home movies of us, then showed the movies the next Sunday. Mother brought surprises and treats for each girl. My brother, Art, came from college and joked with everyone. The other girls looked forward to my family's visits as much as I did.

Friends and neighbors in Austin, hearing about the polio girls who didn't get company, loaded my parents with potato chips and peanuts, brownies and cookies, all of which we stashed under my bed.

Before long I got a wheelchair and learned to push myself around. I named the wheelchair Silver after the horse in the "Lone Ranger." To the dismay of the staff, I learned to make Silver rear on his hind legs. I raced down the hall as fast as I could, then slammed on the brakes, causing the small front wheels to lift off the floor while I balanced on the large rear ones.

The nurses warned me that this was dangerous, but each time the other kids asked me to do my trick, I waited until the grownups were out of sight and then tore down the hall and "popped a wheelie" in front of the door, where my roommates could see me and applaud.

The wheelchair became my ticket to independence. After I learned to get into it and then back into bed by myself, I even passed out cookies in the dark, when we were supposed to be asleep.

On my thirteenth birthday, I sat in Silver and blew out the candles on the chocolate cake that Mother had brought. I had only one wish: to walk by myself.

My physical therapist, Miss Ballard, became my personal cheerleader, encouraging me to stretch and to work at my exercises. She believed I would walk someday, and her confidence made me believe it, too.

The friendship of my roommates also sustained me. We often sang together after lights out at night. We told jokes and teased each other about boyfriends. Alice, Dorothy, Renée, and Shirley seemed like sisters, and the success of one of us became the success of all. When I got walking sticks and said goodbye to Silver, the other girls clapped. Even though none of them would ever get out of their wheelchairs, my progress was a victory against our mutual foe.

Every Sunday Mother brought my homework, so in addition to attending the hospital school for two hours each day, I studied on my own, trying to keep up with my class in Austin. Between schoolwork and physical therapy, my days were full. But not so full that I didn't get homesick once in a while. I especially missed Grandpa, who lived with my family. I missed B.J., too, although he wrote me funny letters, which I read aloud to the other girls. His letters were signed with a muddy paw print.

In February, five months after I moved in with Dorothy, Alice, Renée, and Shirley, I was discharged from the Sheltering Arms. By then I could walk a few steps by myself.

I continued the physical therapy at home, lying on the dining room table while Mother stretched my muscles. I practiced walking, trying each time to go one minute longer.

In April, still using my walking sticks, I returned to school. Eventually I walked alone well enough that I no longer needed the sticks.

The experience of being paralyzed and uprooted

from my family changed me forever and continues to affect me now, half a century later. Polio taught me perseverance. I rejoiced over minor accomplishments and learned that success can come one small step at a time. Because I know that life might change or even end without warning, I appreciate each day. I cherish family and friends, and try to make the most of my time and talents.

{ 3 }

High School Days

While I recovered from polio, I read a lot. The summer after I got home from the hospital, I devoured an entire set of encyclopedias, from *A* to *Z*. I discovered the Louisa May Alcott books and read *Little Women* many times. *Daddy-Long-Legs* by Jean Webster became a favorite.

I had always loved to read, although I don't remember being read to as a child. When I was growing up, I never saw my parents read for pleasure, yet I regularly sneaked a flashlight into bed and read with my head under the covers when I was supposed to be asleep.

On bright summer days, I sat on the couch with my nose in a book until Mother insisted that I "go outside and get some fresh air." Then I stretched out on the grass or in our hammock and read some more.

I remember only one teacher who read aloud to the class. When I was in fourth grade, Miss Beck read us *The Five Little Peppers and How They Grew.* I hung on every word and begged her to read more than one chapter each day. Miss Beck didn't give in to my pleas, but she did encourage me to read other books. My school had no library, so she suggested that I borrow books from the public library.

I took her advice, checked out a copy of *The Five Little Peppers and How They Grew,* and finished it ahead of the class.

I became a regular visitor at the library. My parents let me read whatever I brought home. The only time they disapproved of my reading was when I used my allowance to buy comic books. Mother thought they were a waste of money, but she never forbade me to read them. My favorites were *Little Lulu* and *Archie and His Friends.*

I loved the library so much that I even played library at home. Each of my childhood Raggedy Ann books has a yellowed 3 x 5 card taped on the inside front cover. On the card, written in my childish cursive writing, is the title of the book and lines for the borrower's name and the due date. However, none of those lines were ever filled in. I pretended to be a librarian, but I couldn't bear to lend out my cherished books.

After polio, I read even more because my weakened muscles prevented me from swimming, bike-riding, bowling, and other activities that my friends enjoyed. Most people, including my family, did not yet have television. Radio, movies, board games, and sports provided entertainment.

Although I loved to read, the *Dog Newspaper* had temporarily ended my hope of becoming a writer. That dream did not surface again until I was in high school.

In my junior year, I signed up to work on the *Austin Sentinel,* my school newspaper. My first creative writing was published there. While the other kids wrote teacher interviews and articles about school games, band concerts, and field trips, I wrote an article about how buttons were trying to take over the world. It warned of an elaborate plot for buttons to pop off clothing at important events, all perfectly timed and coordinated by the button leaders.

I will forever be grateful to the *Sentinel*'s advisor for publishing my button piece. Because it was so different from what the school newspaper usually printed, it created a stir. Once again I received congratulations on my writing, and this time the feedback made me think seriously of becoming a writer.

This was not a common goal for a girl growing up in the Midwest in the 1950s. I had never met an author. Since we had no TV, I'd never seen author interviews. Writing instruction in school consisted of lessons in grammar and sentence construction, not creative writing.

Girls were expected to marry and raise families. After my button article was published, I wondered if it might be possible to do both. Could I be a wife and mother *and* an author? I wasn't sure. My mother had never worked outside our home; only one of my friends had a mother with a job.

Besides writing for the *Sentinel*, I volunteered to help with the school yearbook, the *Austinian*. There wasn't much artistic writing involved, but I often stayed after school to do extra work—helping with layouts or writing photo captions. I even sold advertising to local businesses.

Toward the end of my junior year, I had to choose whether to be on the staff of the *Sentinel* or the *Austinian* during my senior year. I chose the *Austinian* because I thought I had a good chance of being named editor. What an honor that would be! Because of my hard work and dedication, I felt I deserved the position, and I looked forward to the day when the announcement would be made.

I rushed into the room that day and read the posted announcement. *Editor: Gary Eppen. Associate Editor: Peg Schulze.*

After I congratulated my friend Gary, I tried to figure out why he was selected. I decided that he must be more competent and smarter than I was, as well as a better writer.

Many years later, when I returned to my high school as a guest speaker, I confided my long-ago disappointment to a former teacher who had come to hear my talk. She told me, "But you could never have been the yearbook editor. Back then they always chose a boy."

Indignation streaked through me like a shooting star.

Perhaps Gary would have been picked anyway—certainly he did a fine job as editor—but it was so unfair. No matter how hard I worked or how good my work was, I could never have been chosen as the editor just because I was a girl.

The sting of not being selected was soothed when I landed my first summer job. Except for a few evenings spent baby-sitting, I had never earned any money, but I was determined to collect my own pay that summer.

All my classmates, plus the graduating seniors and the college students who were home for the summer, were also looking for summer work, so the competition was fierce. Who would hire a girl with no experience and no skills?

Instead of reading the Help Wanted ads, as my friends were doing, I thought about where I would most like to work. I decided that since I wanted to be a writer, the logical job for me would be at the local newspaper.

Gathering up my courage, I walked into the offices of the *Austin Daily Herald* and said I was seeking summer employment. To my amazement, one of the newspaper's owners, Geraldine Rasmussen, agreed to interview me. Mrs. Rasmussen asked why I thought I was qualified to work at the *Herald*.

"I'm not," I admitted, "but I wrote for the school newspaper, and I'm on the staff of the yearbook. I like to read and write."

She asked for some personal references. I gulped. Except for my parents, I couldn't think of a single person who would recommend me for a job of any kind.

"What about your English teacher," Mrs. Rasmussen suggested, "or the teacher who supervises the *Sentinel?*"

I gave both names.

"Wait here," she said. She went to the next room, and I knew she was making a phone call. When she returned she asked, "Have you ever done any proofreading?"

"Yes," I replied. "We always proofread the *Sentinel* before it gets printed, and I helped proofread the *Austinian.*"

She nodded. "I need someone to proofread the *Herald,*" she said. "When can you start?"

"Me?" I asked. "You want to hire *me*?"

She managed not to laugh at my astonishment. "Your teachers recommend you highly."

She told me what hours I would work, and what my pay would be. Elated, I agreed.

I had a job! And not just any old job; I was working at the *Austin Daily Herald.* A newspaper! My feet skimmed the sidewalk as I raced home with the news.

I never found out which of my teachers Mrs. Rasmussen called or what they told her. I can only marvel that she trusted an inexperienced sixteen-year-old to do a job that many adults couldn't handle.

My duty as proofreader was to read the entire newspaper before it went to press and make sure there weren't any mistakes. I read every word of the news stories, the feature stories, the garden club announcements, the classified ads, the sports page, and the obituaries.

I read carefully, with a dictionary close by. I learned a lot about my town that summer, and I also learned the importance of accuracy.

For the first three weeks of the summer, I spotted

every error in time to have it corrected. Then one day I missed a mistake, and it got published.

When I arrived at work the next day, Mrs. Rasmussen was waiting for me. She handed me seven telephone messages—all pointing out that in yesterday's paper the word *accused* was spelled wrong. A copy of the paper lay open on my desk, with the error circled in red. *Accussed*, it said, right there on page six.

I knew there was only one *s* in *accused*, even without using the dictionary. How could I have missed something so obvious?

Humiliated, I apologized for my carelessness and promised to do better. Then I held my breath and stared at my shoes, expecting to be fired.

To my vast relief, Mrs. Rasmussen smiled. "Only one mistake in over three weeks is extraordinary," she told me. "Keep up the good work."

I gaped at her. "I get to stay?"

"You're the best proofreader I've had in years," she replied. "I'll be sorry when school starts and you have to leave. I hope you'll want to come back next summer."

Praise is a far better motivator than shame.

Because I wanted Geraldine Rasmussen's high opinion of my work, I diligently read and reread every word of the *Austin Daily Herald* each day, frequently checking my dictionary. I was determined never, ever to let another mistake slip past my watchful eyes.

The paper was perfect for the rest of the summer.

{ 4 }

Commercials, Cats, and Carl

My senior year blew past like dry leaves on a windy day. Gary and I worked well together, laughed a lot, and were both proud of the 1954 *Austinian*.

By April, with graduation fast approaching, my classmates and I began looking for jobs again. For some, it would now be permanent work. For me, it was another summer job, until I started college.

I planned to call Mrs. Rasmussen and ask for the proofreading job back, but a teacher told me that the local radio station, KAUS, needed someone to write commercials. The station manager had called the school to ask about potential writers, and the teacher thought I would be a good candidate for the job.

I made an appointment for Saturday morning. I ironed my white blouse and dark green skirt, polished my saddle shoes, curled my hair, and tried to look more confident than I felt.

The only thing I remember about the job interview is my excitement at being inside a radio station. This was even better than a newspaper office!

The manager must have asked me questions and I must have answered them, but our conversation has fled my memory. I do remember that before I left KAUS that day, I had agreed to work for two hours after school and three hours every Saturday morning until I graduated. Then I would work full-time all summer until I left in September for the University of Minnesota.

My friends were bowled over by the news. Most of them had jobs scooping ice cream or lifeguarding at the community pool or taking tickets at the Paramount Theater. I loved telling people that I worked as a writer at the radio station. It sounded so sophisticated.

At KAUS, I acquired skills that would serve me well for the rest of my life. I learned to write quickly. The station used a lot of commercials every day, so there was a constant demand for new material.

I also learned to make something out of nothing. The salesmen who sold radio ads to local businesses often didn't tell me much about what was being advertised. It was common for them to hand me a scrap of paper on which a few words were scrawled.

One note, written on the back of a paper napkin, said, "Sale shoes Wall Sat."

This meant that Wallace's Department Store would have a sale on shoes, starting Saturday. It also meant that I was expected to write words so clever and compelling about shoes that everyone in the KAUS listening audience would rush to be at Wallace's Saturday morning, cash in hand.

I needed a constant stream of fresh ideas, and I invented a technique to help generate them. I called this trick "Five Minutes of Nonstop Writing." I still use it and recommend it to students.

I discovered that if I wrote as quickly as possible, without stopping, for at least five minutes, I always thought of an idea that could become a commercial. I bought a kitchen timer and took it to work. I would set the timer for five minutes, and as soon as it began ticking, my fingers flew across the typewriter keys. Sometimes I began by typing, "I don't know what to say; I don't know what to say," but no matter how desperate I was for words, I would not let myself quit typing until that timer rang.

It worked every time. When the five minutes ended, I'd have the germ of an idea that could be worked into a thirty-second or sixty-second commercial.

I wrote about cars, mattresses, clothing, and appliances. I wrote about mortgages and pet food. I made up jingles and invented dialogue.

One ad for a sale on shampoo began like this: "Here is an important warning from the Poetry Association of KAUS.

> The thick white flakes are falling
> though there is no storm alert;
> those drifts are quite appalling:
> they're dandruff on your shirt!"

I found the station's supply of taped sound effects and began adding instructions for background noises of thunder, slamming doors, and howling winds. These sound effects often gave me ideas for new commercials.

One ad opened with the sound of barking dogs. The barking faded into the background as the announcer said, "There are bargains to bark about this week at Cleveland Hardware. You'll howl with happiness when you see the prices on new refrigerators, and best of all, you don't need a license to take advantage of this sale. Be the first in your pack to sniff out the low prices." The commercial ended with more barking.

My simple word plays and silly ideas made people chuckle, and the commercials got rerun many times.

The more I wrote, the more confident I became, and the more I loved the work. It was great to get a paycheck every Friday, but I was having so much fun that the money quickly became secondary to the writing.

While I felt like a beginner, the salesmen, the announcers, the secretary, and the one full-time writer all treated me as if I belonged in their elite group. They expected me to do well, and I tried my best to deserve their confidence.

I began the job as an inexperienced high school senior. When I left for the University of Minnesota that fall, I was a competent and prolific writer.

During my high school years, I began a friend-ship with a boy named Carl Kehret (pronounced *carrot*). I met Carl when I agreed to sell barbecued hamburgers, called lushburgers, at my church's stand at the county fair. He had signed up to work at the same time. We liked each other immediately, and when our shift ended we strolled the fair-grounds together, picking up discarded glass pop bottles to be recycled.

We began to date. He had an old Plymouth car with a horn that went "Oooga-oooga." He often cruised past my house and tooted that horn. He sometimes arrived in one of the milk delivery trucks from his dad's dairy, and occasionally he showed up on horseback. Once he clattered down the street perched on a large yellow tractor. I never knew what to expect, and that was one of the reasons I liked him.

He attended college one hundred miles from home while I was still in high school, but our friend-ship continued in letters and weekend visits. Although I dated a few other boys, they never measured up to Carl. I asked him to come home from college to take me to the junior prom, and again for my senior prom.

Each summer, and during his winter and spring breaks, we spent more time with each other. We played golf, took long drives, had picnics, and went to movies.

One afternoon he drove me to his family's dairy farm and parked beside the cow pasture.

"It's time you learned about cows," he told me.

We walked to the center of the pasture and sat down in the grass. "Hold still and don't say anything," Carl whispered.

We sat silently. Soon the curious cows approached, swishing their tails and watching us with big brown eyes. Before long, we were completely circled by beautiful Golden Guernseys who munched the grass, stared at us, and mooed softly.

I was enchanted, both by the cows and by the young man who had given me such a unique experience.

We never ran out of things to talk about, and because we had the same sense of humor, we laughed a lot, too.

Late one night I heard music outside my bedroom window. When I looked out, I saw Carl in my front yard with an old wind-up phonograph. As he cranked the handle, it played a recording of the song "Peg O' My Heart." What girl wouldn't fall in love?

By the time I finished high school, we knew we wanted to spend the rest of our lives together, and at the end of my freshman year in college, we got married. I was eighteen years old; he was twenty-one.

Once married, it seemed vital for me to cook and keep house, but unnecessary to earn a college degree. Girls at that time were expected to be home-makers, and that's what I decided to be. When I thought about writing, it seemed an impossible fantasy.

I knew how to cook only two things: grilled cheese sandwiches and fudge. As soon as we returned to Austin from our honeymoon, I bought a cookbook. Fortunately, anyone who can read can cook, and I soon had success with spaghetti, cinnamon rolls, and lemon pie.

I could have continued my college education. At the time I didn't want to, a choice I now regret. My husband had a bachelor of science degree and a job at his family's dairy. I was busy baking chocolate-chip cookies.

Carl and I adopted a kitten, Stompy. Although I had always considered myself a dog person, I quickly fell in love with this small gray cat.

After a few months of housekeeping, I returned to work at the radio station.

One of the KAUS salesmen, Ken Soderberg, had blond good looks and a sharp wit. I was in awe of all the KAUS employees, but I felt especially tongue-tied around Ken. He taught me something even more valuable than how to write quickly and create ideas out of nothing.

One afternoon Carl was riding in a milk truck when a car ran into it. His left elbow was broken and he had to stay in the hospital for surgery.

That night Stompy didn't come home. All night long, with Carl gone, I called Stompy and searched our yard with a flashlight.

As soon as it grew light the next morning, I found her—dead on the side of the road behind our house.

Broken-hearted, I ran to my neighbor and told him the terrible news. The neighbor, a farmer who had raised livestock for decades, said, "It's only a cat. Be glad it wasn't Carl."

He didn't mean to be unkind; many people then and now think animals are unimportant.

It's only a cat.

But she wasn't just a cat! She was Stompy, my special little friend, and I mourned her deeply.

I was supposed to go to work at KAUS that morning, but after I buried Stompy, I couldn't stop crying. I considered calling in sick. I toyed with saying I needed to be at the hospital with Carl, but I couldn't bring myself to lie to the colleagues who'd been so kind to me.

In the end, I called the station, and when Ken Soderberg answered, I blubbered, "I can't come to work. My cat got run over!" Then I dissolved in tears.

I braced myself for Ken's reprimand, waiting for him to say Stompy was only a cat and if I wanted to keep my job, I had better get myself down to the station.

Ken's voice was gentle. "I'm so sorry," he said. "A pet is one of the family, and of course you can't work today. Don't worry about it. Grieve for your cat, and come back to work when you're ready."

It was my first experience with someone who understood my affinity with animals. Now I know that many people adore their dogs and cats and horses and guinea pigs, but I didn't know that then.

During visiting hours that afternoon, I sat beside Carl's hospital bed and told him what had happened to Stompy. We held hands and cried together. One reason I have always loved my husband so much is that he has a tender heart. He cries as easily as I do, and his love for animals runs as deep.

When I went to work the next morning, a bouquet of flowers from Ken's garden brightened my desk.

I don't know if I ever told Ken how much I was touched by his sympathy and understanding. I hope I did. I have followed his example many times when friends have lost a beloved animal.

Carl and I soon adopted another cat (Tiger, who lived to be fourteen), and since then we have never been without one or more companion animals.

{ 5 }

Two Letters That
Changed My Life

Three years after our marriage, Carl and I moved from Minnesota to California. My dad had been transferred to Fresno, California, two years earlier, and after we visited my parents we wanted to live on the West Coast, too. Carl was hired by a large company, and I got a job with an employment agency. I interviewed available workers, then matched them with employers who needed temporary help. I worked there a year, and left the day I became a mother.

When the doctor told me that because of polio, I couldn't have a baby, Carl and I knew we wanted to adopt. Our adoption agency did a thorough "home study" to be sure we could provide a good home for a child. We were interviewed separately and together, and a social worker visited our home twice. During one visit, she asked me, "If you never have a child, will your life be happy?"

I answered, "Yes," then worried that I had blown our chances. I wanted a baby, but if we didn't get one I wouldn't waste my life yearning for what I couldn't have.

Bob came to us when he was five weeks old. I was at work when our social worker called. "We have a baby boy for you," she told me.

I burst into tears. When I calmed down enough, I set a time for the following day when we could see the baby, learn about his background, and decide if he was right for us. As if we would have said no!

As soon as I finished talking to the social worker, I called Carl. The next morning we met our son.

No young couple ever appreciated parenthood more than we did. While Carl was at work, I pushed the stroller on long walks, hung diapers to dry in the sun, and rocked my baby to sleep. Evenings and weekends, Carl took baby pictures, and we both marveled at every new thing Bob did.

Carl got transferred twice, so we moved when

Bob was eighteen months old and again six months later. In between moves, we applied to the adoption agency for another baby.

Anne was two months old when she joined our family. We had just bought an old house, and our electricity could not be turned on until the wiring was repaired. Carl was in the basement with the county electrical inspector, finding out what needed to be fixed.

Once again, I answered the phone. The same social worker told me that the agency had a daughter for us.

I flew down the basement stairs shouting, "We have a baby girl!" Carl and I cried and hugged, and then explained to the startled electrical inspector, who not only joined the celebration, but turned our power on. "You need to be able to sterilize baby bottles," he said. "I trust you to make the repairs."

I loved being a mother, and enjoyed my kids at every age: babies, toddlers, schoolchildren, and teenagers. Now I'm repeating the fun with my grandchildren.

After Bob and Anne were in school all day, I grew restless. I learned to sew, I knitted sweaters, and I read a lot. I was the Cub Scout den mother, I volunteered at the school library, and I helped a non-profit theater group, but I still felt incomplete, like a book with missing pages.

One day I received a letter from the University of Minnesota. It was a survey of intellectually gifted students who had dropped out of school. "What are you doing now?" the survey asked. "Have you won any awards?"

That letter zapped me like a lightning bolt. *Intellectually gifted?* No one had ever told me that. I had always felt smart, but I thought everyone felt that way. *Had I won any awards?* For what? I had a blue ribbon from the county fair for my lemon pie, but I knew that wasn't the kind of award the university meant.

I reread the letter several times. Then I asked myself what I wanted in my future. If I got this same letter ten years down the road, what answers would I give?

The next day, I enrolled in a California community college. The application form had a space to put down what future career I had in mind. I thought about putting "writer," but that seemed too impossible. I didn't want to leave the space blank, so I wrote "unsure."

I signed up to study astronomy, comparative religions, and early childhood education. I also took a class called "composition and reading."

I liked school even more as an adult than I had as a teenager. In the composition and reading class, the professor had us write a one-thousand-word paper each week. This quickly became my favorite course. I loved writing those papers, and I thrived on the professor's encouragement.

When our beloved cat died, I wrote about him. The professor read my paper aloud in class, and I saw tears on the cheeks of my classmates. None of them had known Tiger, yet they wept at his loss because my words had touched them.

This is what I want to do, I thought. I want to write. I want to share my thoughts and emotions by creating stories. When I registered for the next semester, I stated my career goal without hesitation: writer.

After I had completed only two semesters, Carl's company went out of business in California. We moved to Washington State, where he had a new job.

I called a local college and learned that I'd be considered an out-of-state student for one year, even though Washington was now my home. We couldn't afford the higher tuition that out-of-state students must pay, so once again my college education was put aside.

Since my goal, after getting my degree, was to be a writer, I decided that I would spend the year writing. It would be good practice.

As soon as Bob and Anne left for school each morning, I headed for my desk in our unfinished basement. Most days, except for lunch and a break to walk George, our dog, I stayed there until the kids returned home in the afternoon.

I subscribed to two magazines for writers, and I bought a copy of *Writer's Market*, a book that tells how to submit writing to publishers. I began sending magazine articles and short stories to potential publishers. My goal was to put a new piece of writing in the mail every Friday.

I made a chart to keep track of my many submissions, all of which came back with brief letters declining my work. Most of these letters, which writers call rejection slips, said simply, "Sorry."

Not as sorry as I am, I thought. A few said, "Not right for us." Why not? I wondered. What's wrong?

Except for Carl, Anne, and Bob, I didn't tell anyone that I was submitting my work. I was too afraid that I would never publish anything, and I didn't want others to know of my failure. It's hard enough to be rejected without announcing it to the world.

As the months went by, though, I began to think of myself as a writer anyway. When a new friend asked what I did, I said, "I'm a writer," and I knew it was true. Getting published didn't make me a writer. It was the act of sitting at my typewriter day after day, putting words on paper.

With every submission, I included a stamped envelope addressed to myself so that if the editor didn't want to publish my work, it could be returned to me. When I got my mail each day, I glanced through it, dreading the sight of one of those self-addressed envelopes. They always meant a rejection.

Bob often mispronounced words when he was growing up. One day he brought in the mail, handed me one of the all-too-familiar self-addressed envelopes, and said sadly, "Sorry, Momma. It's another dejection slip."

He was right. I did get discouraged, but even so the process of writing daily and submitting my work became my way of life. When the year ended and I could once again afford to go to college, I didn't do it. It would have taken too much time away from my work, from my new life as a writer.

I continued to write, submit my work, and have it returned—until one special day in 1972 when I got a different kind of letter from a publisher.

It was an ordinary Saturday. As I carried in the mail, I looked, as always, for one of my self-addressed envelopes. When I saw one, I laid it aside with the bills. I didn't want to spoil a happy morning with my family by reading another "dejection" slip.

Later, I finally opened the envelope. Instead of a returned manuscript, it contained a letter from a small magazine called *Today's Christian Mother.* My short article, "Whistle While You Wait," had been accepted for publication. Payment of five dollars would follow.

Goosebumps tingled up my arms and the back of my neck. My hands shook as I read the letter again, and then again.

"I sold an article!" I yelled. "To a magazine!"

Carl and the kids came running.

"I sold a magazine article," I repeated, in case they hadn't heard me the first time.

I was as thrilled as if the pay had been five thousand dollars. The editor of a magazine liked what I had written well enough to publish it. At last it was official: I was a published writer!

"How much are they paying you?" Carl asked.

"Five dollars. I'm going to save it until I earn enough for all of us to go to Hawaii."

To his everlasting credit, my husband did not suggest that five dollars was a drop in the ocean as far as the cost of a trip to Hawaii went. Instead he said, "Good plan."

As soon as the check arrived, I went to the bank and opened my Hawaii account. The minimum amount needed to open a new savings account was five dollars. I had just made it.

{ 6 }

Twenty-five Words or Less

The savings account grew slowly, partly because I tried too many different kinds of writing. Instead of deciding what I most wanted to write and then working to improve, I wrote a little of almost everything. I tried poetry, humor, short stories, and nonfiction, all aimed at adult readers.

Writing is like practicing a musical instrument: the more you do it, the better you get. However, my early years of writing were like practicing the piano one week, the violin the next week, and the banjo the week after that. I jumped from fiction to nonfiction, from prose to poetry, without ever gaining expertise in any one kind of writing.

Although my rejections still far outnumbered my acceptances, I did publish a few more short pieces. I lacked focus, but I was persistent. I tried to write five pages every day.

After that first article to *Today's Christian Mother,* I sold a humor article about Thanksgiving, "Feast or Football," to *Deli News,* a publication which went to small food businesses.

Next I sold a verse about Washington's wet weather to a newsletter put out by the American Automobile Association.

My dad subscribed to the *Wall Street Journal,* a business newspaper, and I always chuckled at the funny verse in its "Pepper and Salt" column. I began sending my light verse to the *Wall Street Journal,* and in the next few years they published four of my poems.

My biggest sale that first year was a six-page short story about a beloved childhood doll. It was published by a Baptist magazine, *Home Life.*

After a full year of writing five days a week, six hours a day, I had a grand total of $97.50 in my Hawaii account. Most workers who get paid less than seven cents an hour would be unhappy, but I was elated whenever a piece of writing got published, and those small acceptances made me keep trying.

For Mother's Day that year, Anne gave me a painting she had done of two palm trees on a beach —to encourage me to get to Hawaii, she said. The painting still hangs in my office, a reminder not only of the path I've walked as a writer, but also of my good fortune in having a daughter who understands my dreams.

It finally dawned on me that I might have more success at hitting the target if I narrowed my aim. I made a list of the three magazines I most wanted to see my work published in. The *Writer* topped my list. I read every word of that magazine each month, paying close attention to the advice from professional writers. Someday I hoped to be a successful writer who could give pointers to beginners.

Next on my list was the *Reader's Digest* because it published many inspirational articles of the kind I was trying to write.

The third magazine I chose was *Good Housekeeping.* My mother subscribed to it, and so did I. I enjoyed its short stories and its articles about family life.

When I sat down to write each day, I tried to aim for the *Reader's Digest* with nonfiction and *Good Housekeeping* with fiction. This helped me slant my material, but even so my Hawaii account grew slowly.

One night I saw a newspaper ad for a large department store. The ad said, "Win a Trip to Hawaii! Write twenty-five words or less on Why I Want to Go to Hawaii, and you could win a trip for two, all expenses paid."

My pulse raced. This should be a snap, I thought. I'm a writer, and I want to go to Hawaii. Surely I could think of twenty-five words to say. I grabbed a pencil and a piece of paper. Twenty-five words? In no time I had a couple of hundred words, which is when I realized that a good contest entry might be trickier than I thought. I began the slow process of condensing long phrases into short ones and eliminating unnecessary words.

I spent that evening and all of the next day composing my masterpiece. I don't remember exactly what I said, but I know I used words like "aloha" and "beach" and "pineapple." I copied my entry carefully on clean paper, drove to the store that was sponsoring the contest, and put it in a large box just inside the entrance. The box already overflowed with several hundred other entries. My confidence melted away. I returned home, sat at my desk, and began to write yet another short story. If I didn't win the contest, perhaps I could sell the story and add the payment to my Hawaii account.

Two weeks later, the phone call came. I had won! The trip was for only two people, but I asked if Carl and I could pay for our children and take them along. The store manager said we could.

The trip cleaned out my writing account and made a big dent in our family savings, but all four of us spent a marvelous week in Hawaii. We toured a pineapple factory and visited the Pearl Harbor memorial. We drove around Oahu in a jitney. We spent hours each day on the wonderful beaches.

Throughout that week, I glowed with the knowledge that this happened because I was a writer. My creativity had earned this wonderful vacation for us! That awareness enhanced everything I did each day and sang me to sleep every night.

When we got home, I returned to my daily writing schedule, but I wondered if there might be other contests where the contestants had to write something in order to win. If the prize went to someone whose name was randomly selected, I didn't bother to enter. I wanted to earn the prize with words.

Before long I read about a dog food company's contest. Entrants were asked to write fifty words about "Why My Dog Is Worth Her Weight in Gold." Well! I had been writing about my wonderful animals ever since the *Dog Newspaper* when I was ten years old.

The first-prize winner would receive an ounce of gold for each pound that his or her dog weighed. I carried George, our part-Pekinese, part-Cairn terrier, part-unknown to our bathroom scale. Sixteen pounds. Wishing George were a Saint Bernard, I started to write.

If I won first place, I planned to stuff George with dog treats prior to his weigh-in and then use my winnings as the down payment on a new car, which we badly needed.

I poured my love for George into that entry, but the first prize went to someone else.

However, a few weeks after the contest closed, our mailman knocked on the door with a package.

I tore it open and learned that I had won *second* place. I lifted out my prize: a Krugerrand, a one-ounce gold coin of the Republic of South Africa.

The Krugerrand was shiny and pretty, but I wasn't sure what I would do with it. It was barely heavy enough to be a paperweight. Still, it meant a contest judge somewhere had liked my writing, and that knowledge was the real prize.

A few days after the gold coin arrived, Carl called me from work and said, "I found a company that buys precious metal. If you want to sell your coin, they'll give you six hundred and fourteen dollars for it."

Six hundred and fourteen dollars! It wouldn't buy a car, but I could keep myself in typewriter ribbons, paper, and postage for a long time with that much money. The next day I parted with my piece of gold.

I bought a subscription to a newsletter for people who enter contests as a hobby. Through this source, I learned of several other writing-type contests.

I won a slow-cooker pot from the American Dairy Association by writing why milk is good for you. I won a clothes dryer by writing a poem about why I needed one, and after toiling over twenty-five words about "Why I Like Shasta Pop," I won the chance to run through a grocery store for five minutes. Anything I could put in the cart in five minutes was mine!

On the morning of my race through the supermarket, Carl stayed home from work and we kept Anne (a fourth-grader) and Bob (a sixth-grader) out of school for a couple of hours so that they could go along.

I wore my best tennis shoes. The store manager, who seemed almost as pleased as I was, greeted me with a lovely corsage of white carnations. Then he started the timer, and I was off.

"Get cases of Twinkies!" yelled Bob.

"Root beer! Candy bars!" shouted Anne.

Apparently my children thought the purpose of the prize was to load my shopping cart with all the treats I would normally never buy.

When my five minutes were up, I had two grocery carts heaped with nutritious food plus enough Twinkies, candy bars, and root beer to keep my children happy for months.

This exciting morning gave me much more than free groceries. It validated my skill as a writer.

I've always loved baseball, and so has Carl. Bob is an even bigger fan than we are. During the fourteen years that we lived in the San Francisco Bay Area, we saw many Giants' games at Candlestick Park. When we moved to Washington State in 1970, we sorely missed having a professional baseball team to cheer for, so when Seattle got an American League franchise in 1977 we went to the very first Seattle Mariners' game. We've been Mariners' fans ever since.

One April night when Bob and Anne were in high school, we attended a Mariners' game. As the fans entered the Kingdome, each was handed a printed flyer. I read mine after we were seated and could hardly concentrate on the game.

The Seattle Mariners were having a contest! They wanted people to write twenty-five words or less on "Why I Love Baseball." The first prize, a cruise to Mexico, didn't interest me a whole lot, but there were twenty-three other prizes of season tickets to the Mariners' games. Bob's eyes sparkled as he pointed to that line. "Go for it, Momma," he urged.

As always, I spent several hours composing my entry. Because I was a true baseball fan, I knew the lingo. This is what I wrote: "Baseball gives me steals and deals, fouls and howls, umps and slumps, beers and cheers, frills and thrills, hitters and spitters—and I love it!"

When the winners were announced, the Kehret household celebrated. My entry had won season tickets! I received my prize, as did the other winners, in the Kingdome before a game. I walked out to home plate, accepted my tickets, and had my picture taken with one of the players. I carried a baseball for Bob, and several players autographed it. What fun we had that summer, cheering for our favorite team.

A neighbor who learned of my prizes commented, "You're always winning something. You're so lucky!"

But it wasn't luck; it was hard work. Each contest entry took hours of creative effort. I wrote and rewrote jingles, I revised each sentence dozens of times, I experimented with and abandoned countless ideas. For a contest entry, every word is crucial, and a short sentence must be as effective as a long one.

One day a friend called to tell me there was a contest on the back of the Kraft Macaroni and Cheese Dinner box. The grand prize was a new car.

"Is it a lottery-type contest," I asked, "or do you have to write something in order to win?" She couldn't remember.

Since we still needed a car, I immediately bought a box of Kraft Macaroni and Cheese Dinner. The contest was what I had hoped for: "In twenty-five words or less complete the statement, 'I Like Kraft Macaroni and Cheese Dinner because...'"

According to the rules, winners would be chosen on the basis of "originality, aptness of thought, and sincerity of expression." Since originality was mentioned first, I was determined to come up with a fresh, new idea, something that would make my entry stand out from the thousands of others.

I labored long and hard. My entry was different from anything I'd done before, and I used exactly twenty-five words. The concept was original, the words were appropriate, and no contestant could have been more sincere. My family really did like Kraft Macaroni and Cheese Dinners, and it was a good thing because the more time I spent at my desk, the less I spent in the kitchen.

Entries had to be received by December 1, 1978. I mailed mine on September 25, to be sure it arrived in time. The rules said that winners would be notified within thirty days of when the contest closed. That meant I should hear by New Year's Eve. Maybe they'll do it a little early, I thought. What a great Christmas gift a new car would be! That didn't happen, but I still believed I would win because I knew it was the most creative entry I'd ever written.

When New Year's Day, 1979, came and went with no word from Kraft, I lost hope of winning that new car. The fresh, creative idea that I'd been so excited about had not even merited one of the runner-up prizes.

But on January 8th, I received a letter saying I was a finalist and enclosing a form for me to sign, stating that my entry was my own work.

My hopes soared as I mailed the form back.

I was jittery for the rest of the week. Each day I rushed to the mailbox as soon as the mail was delivered, hoping for a letter from Kraft.

Nine days later, I got a phone call. I had won the grand prize! I screamed and jumped up and down.

I called Carl at work. "I won the car!" I yelled. "I won the car!"

I ran across the street and told my neighbor. I called the friend who had let me know about the contest and made a date to treat her to lunch. I could barely wait for Bob and Anne to get home from school so I could tell them. I told George at least ten times, and he always wagged his tail.

Two weeks later, I drove home from the car dealership in my brand new white Honda Civic. How I loved that car! It was fun to drive, got great gas mileage, and represented all my hopes and dreams of being a successful writer. I drove it until Anne graduated from college; then we gave it to her as a graduation gift, and she drove it for several years more.

Here is my winning entry: I like Kraft Macaroni and Cheese Dinner because...

it solves my menu puzzle.

1	2	3	4	5	6	7	8	9	10	11	12	13	14
		H	A	N	D	Y							
			U		U							Q	
	B	E	S	T	M		F				L	U	
			R		G		A				U	A	
	D	E	L	I	C	I	O	U	S		S	L	
	E		T		O		T				C	I	
	P		I		D			P			I	T	
	E	N	J	O	Y		S	A	V	O	R	Y	
	N		U				L				U		
	D		S	U	P	E	R		A		S		
	A	D							T		T		
	B	A	R	G	A	I	N		A		A		
	L	O							B	L	I	S	S
	E	C	O	N	O	M	I	C	A	L		T	
		L							E	A	S	Y	

{ 7 }

Pretending to Be Someone Else

My contest prizes came over a period of twelve years. During that time, I continued to write five pages daily and submit stories and articles. Gradually, I had fewer "dejections" and more acceptance letters.

Because I love theater, I tried writing skits and one-act plays. When a few were published, I wrote more. I also kept writing both fiction and nonfiction for religious magazines such as *Home Life*, the *Christian Herald*, and *Catholic Digest*.

One summer I went to the Pacific Northwest Writers' Conference. On the first day, I intended to go to a panel on marketing but got lost on campus and ended up in the wrong building. I didn't realize my mistake until the session started.

I thought it would have been rude to get up and leave, so instead of the panel on marketing, I heard a panel on writing for magazines such as *True Confessions, True Experience,* and *True Story.* I had never read any of these magazines but since I was stuck in the wrong room, I listened to what the panel members said. I learned that these magazines publish stories written from the first-person viewpoint, as if the events of the story had happened to the narrator. Most of the stories were about family problems, the same sort of story I was writing.

"But don't the stories have to be true?" someone in the audience asked.

"The writer must sign a statement that the story is *based* on truth," one of the writers explained. "That's a pretty broad statement. Usually I base my stories on something I read in the newspaper."

That's what I do, I thought, only I sell my stories about family problems to religious magazines.

"The pay ranges from three cents to five cents per word, depending on the magazine," one of the speakers said.

That got my attention! I usually received either a half-cent or one cent per word for my stories.

When I got home, I bought copies of the magazines the panel had talked about and read them from cover to cover. I sent for their writer's guidelines.

Then I wrote a story about how I accidentally saw my son stealing money from my purse. Bob had not done this, of course, but the story was based on truth; a former neighbor had once asked my advice about this situation.

It was a family story with a moral, exactly what I had been writing all along, only this time, instead of submitting it to one of the religious magazines, I sent it to *True Experience*, where it sold for three cents per word.

My story was titled "My Son Was a Thief," and Bob was outraged until I pointed out that my name did not appear in the magazine.

All the stories in *True Experience* were published without a byline, the phrase that tells who the author is, such as "by Peg Kehret." Also, I had the good sense to name the son in the story something other than Bob.

Thus began my years of imagining myself in someone else's shoes. I wrote about family problems, medical problems, and social problems. In the process, I learned to write fiction that was based on true events.

Because all of these stories were written from the first-person viewpoint, as if they had really happened to me, my family and friends teased me about all the peculiar things I had supposedly experienced. I loved pretending to be other people. It was like being an actress without the stage fright.

I became caught up in each of my characters so that they seemed real to me. I often thought about them, mentally revising the story, even when I was far from my typewriter.

Once we were driving along in ninety-degree heat when Carl glanced over at me and said, "Are you *cold*? You're shivering!"

"I'm writing about someone whose car plunges into an icy river," I explained.

He just shook his head.

Because there were no bylines, I could write as many stories as I wanted. Ideas floated through my mind like flakes in a snow globe that's been vigorously shaken, and I often had more than one story in the same magazine. One unforgettable issue of

True Confessions contained five of my stories.

This meant I had to imagine myself in the minds and bodies of five very different people. Here are the five people I pretended to be that month:

1. A teenager guilty of a hit-and-run accident.
2. A middle-aged woman who had the only matching kidney for her sister, who needed a transplant. But the sisters had not spoken for years.
3. A young mother whose baby had a disease that causes bones to break easily.
4. A black grandmother who was selected by a white family for an Adopt-a-Grandmother program. (That idea came from an article in the *New York Times*. The editor of *True Confessions* sent it to me along with a note saying, "Maybe this would make a story.")
5. A construction worker who found a large sum of money inside the walls of a building he was demolishing. He had to decide whether to keep it to pay his son's medical bills or turn it over to the building's owner.

Five stories in one issue! My imagination worked

overtime as I envisioned having problem after problem. All of the stories had sound morals, and I was proud of them.

I especially liked to read the "Letters to the Editor" pages in the magazines because readers often wrote to say that one of my stories had helped them solve a similar problem.

One summer I wrote my way through the medical shelf of my public library. Besides the kidney transplant and the brittle bone disease, I wrote about having a heart attack, getting my leg amputated, and refusing to vaccinate my children. On paper, I had a different ailment every week.

I was careful to verify any medical information that I used, either by reading medical journals or by asking questions of my own doctor. But I wrote less about the disease itself than about the feelings of the people involved. I knew what it was like to be sick and afraid. I knew how it felt to lie helpless in a hospital bed. I could write convincingly about people who had those feelings.

As I crafted these stories, I learned to create characters who had believable motivations for their actions. The dialogue had to be realistic. Each story needed conflict and suspense. The more stories I wrote, the more confident I became.

The same editor who sometimes sent suggestions for stories asked if I would write a serial. She wanted a chapter a month for seven months.

I dove right in with a mystery about a haunted house. Telling the story in seven chapters taught me how to write a novel. Each chapter had to have a suspenseful ending that would make the readers want to buy the next issue. Later, when I began to write novels for children, this experience helped me craft the "cliff-hanger" chapter endings that readers love.

A child once grumbled to me, "Why do you always quit right in the good parts?"

I laughed. I do it on purpose, and I learned how by practicing day after day.

At home in LaCrosse, Wisconsin, age three.

A father-daughter piano duet.

My favorite activity, age eight.

*B. J., age six, and me, age fifteen,
at our house in Austin, Minnesota.*

My graduation picture from Austin
High School, Class of 1954.

Our wedding—July 2, 1955.
Carl and I don't feel sentimental when we see this
picture; we laugh, because we remember what I was
saying: "Watch out! You're stepping on my dress!"

My parents with Carl, Anne, Bob
(holding George), and me in 1972.

In front of our motor home with Daisy.
It took us across the country many times, visiting
schools, libraries, and bookstores where
I gave talks or did signings.

*Pete and Molly checking out the campground
from the motor home window and resting up
for the three A.M. "Cat Follies."*

When I arrived at schools to give talks,
"Welcome" signs always pleased me.

Carl and me at the humane society with the
January 1989 Pet of the Month.

Receiving the Young Hoosier Award (1992),
my first children's choice award, from Nancy McGriff,
Association of Indiana Media Educators. What a thrill!

In my study with Small Steps *and other books.*

{ 8 }

Cheers and Tears

After attending a workshop at a mental health clinic, I wrote an article on how to overcome depression and sold it to *Good Housekeeping.* I had finally accomplished one of my magazine goals. After publishing more than two hundred anonymous stories, I liked seeing my byline in *Good Housekeeping,* and I did some serious thinking about my career.

By then I was averaging one anonymous story per week and selling everything I wrote. Most of my stories were five thousand words long, so I was earning a decent amount and having fun as well.

Yet I knew it wasn't enough. I wanted to see my work in print, but I also wanted recognition. Publishing without a byline was no way to become known as a writer.

My one-act plays and skits were doing well, so I decided to try a full-length play. Two weeks of every month, I wrote stories to earn some money. The rest of the time I worked on a play with a subplot about a girl who entered contests. (Years later, I used contests again in the novel *Saving Lilly*.)

A local dinner theater produced my play before it was published, which was useful to me as I polished the script.

I wrote three more full-length plays and many short skits while I continued to do anonymous stories.

One of the plays, *Spirit!*, is about an elderly woman in a nursing home who gets in trouble for hosting poker parties and ordering pizza. *Spirit!* won the Forest Roberts Playwriting Award from Northern Michigan University. Part of the prize was a trip to Michigan to see the performance.

I flew to Michigan for three exciting days. The cast and director met me at the airport, all wearing

T-shirts advertising my play. On our way to the campus, we passed a big community reader board. It said, WELCOME PEG KEHRET, WINNING PLAYWRIGHT. I had the driver stop on the side of the road so I could hop out and take a picture.

I sat in the auditorium on opening night, overwhelmed as the people of my imagination walked around on stage, speaking the words I had written for them. The audience laughed at the funny lines and wiped away tears at the poignant ending.

During the curtain call, there were cries of "Author! Author!" As I went forward to take a bow, I thought, This is what it feels like to be a successful writer. Never again would I be satisfied to write anonymously.

If I stopped writing the stories, I would give up a steady source of income. But by then I wanted my name on my writing more than I wanted it on a check.

I asked myself this question: If you knew it would get published, what would you write?

My answer was, a novel. Fiction was fun to write, and I had especially enjoyed telling a story in more than one chapter. I imagined how it would feel to hold in my hands a book that I had written.

It took me a year to write an adult mystery titled *The Ransom at Blackberry Bridge*. With high hopes, I sent it to a literary agent in New York. Many writers have agents who submit their work to publishing companies for them and handle business details with publishers.

My novel came back with a letter from the agent. She said, "You write well, but your heroine seems awfully young. Have you ever considered writing for children?"

I spent another four months revising the book, turning it into a mystery for kids. I made many mistakes during this process. The biggest one was that I did not read any current young adult or middle-grade fiction; I just plowed ahead on my own. When I finished the book the second time, the agent agreed to represent me.

While I waited for her to sell my novel, I wrote another play. Soon after it was published, the agent returned my novel, along with a list of all the publishers who had turned it down.

I stood in my kitchen clutching that list while tears streamed down my cheeks. It had taken me a year to write a novel, and it was not going to be published. Maybe I should give up writing, I thought, and get a "real" job.

I had made that mistake before. Once I had gotten a real estate license. I sold two condominiums, loathed every second of it, and quit. Later I took a part-time position at City Hall, intending to work there half of each day and write the other half. By the time I got dressed up and drove to City Hall, the part-time job took most of the day, and I got little writing done. When I left that job, I felt as if I'd been released from prison.

I knew I could never be happy doing any work except writing, yet I was so discouraged over my unsold book that the next day I signed up as a temporary office worker. I was asked to type bills for an elevator company. The job lasted three days, which was two-and-a-half days too long for me. By noon on the first day, I ached to be home writing.

None of these jobs were unpleasant or difficult; they just didn't excite me. When I write, I'm challenged, wholly engaged, and have a sense of doing important work. Hours pass without my realizing it.

There is great satisfaction in imagining people,

places, and situations, and then writing about them in a way that makes them seem real to others. When I write, I pour my own thoughts, feelings, fears, hopes, and ideals into the pages. Because I write about things that matter to me, my own voice speaks from my work even when I write fiction.

After three days of typing bills, I admitted that I would forever be a writer. My novel had not sold, but at least I had written it. I had done my best, and that was better than not trying. How I use my time is more crucial than how much I earn. From then on I did the work I loved and never again took a "real" job.

I was fortunate to have this choice. Carl made enough money for our family to live on, and he enthusiastically supported my writing efforts. Even in the years when I published little, he believed in my work and encouraged me.

Writers need time to experiment with ideas and words, time to concentrate on a manuscript, time to revise, time to daydream. My husband gave me the luxury of time to write.

I longed to write a second novel for children, but decided I should stick to what I did well. I didn't want to waste another year on a book that wouldn't get published.

The editor of a new magazine called *Woman's World* told me she would publish one short story in each issue and asked if I would like to submit something.

I wrote a story about a young woman who ignores her likable but ordinary boyfriend because she dreams of marrying the star player of the New York Yankees. When I saw " 'Major League Love' by Peg Kehret" in a national magazine, I bought ten copies and gave them to family and friends.

I wrote many more stories for *Woman's World* and all said "by Peg Kehret." I also wrote stories and poems for children's magazines.

One day I got out the chart that I used to keep track of my submissions and realized that my system might help other writers. I wrote "Something in the Mail Every Friday"—and made my first sale to the *Writer.* Another of my magazine goals got checked off.

I never did sell an article to the *Reader's Digest,* but when I opened an unexpected letter from them, out dropped a check. They had reprinted one of the verses I had originally sold to the *Wall Street Journal.*

I laughed as I crossed off the third and final magazine on my list of goals. It had not happened the way I expected, but that was okay. A sale is a sale!

{ 9 }

Alzheimer's Disease

When I was little, I called him Daddy. Later he was Dad. That changed to Father when I was fifteen. It started as a joke, but the joke became an affectionate nickname that stuck, and Art and I called him Father from then on.

"Father" sounds formal and old-fashioned, while my dad was easygoing and full of fun—until he was sixty-two, and diagnosed with Alzheimer's disease. This horrible disease robbed him of his memory, his personality, and his ability to care for himself. It changed not only his life, but my mother's life and the lives of everyone in my family.

When Father was diagnosed, few people knew

anything about Alzheimer's disease. There were no books to inform families how this devastating illness progresses, so I decided to write one.

The difficult research absorbed and exhausted me. I spent days in the University of Washington medical library, reading articles intended for doctors. I interviewed doctors who studied the brain, psychiatrists, and families of patients. I visited a hospital that had an entire ward of Alzheimer's patients, and toured nursing homes. It took me a year.

When the book was finished, I sent it to the agent who had been unable to sell *The Ransom at Blackberry Bridge.* She returned the manuscript. She was not interested in a book about a disease she had never heard of, and she didn't think any publishers would want to read it, either.

I decided to market it myself. I sent it to a university press, where an editor liked it and asked for some revisions. Encouraged, I plunged into the rewrites.

Before I finished, an excellent book called *The 36 Hour Day,* aimed at family members who care for people with Alzheimer's disease, was published.

My editor decided there was no need for a second book on the subject. I put my manuscript away. By the time it became clear that Alzheimer's disease was far more common than first thought, and other books on the subject would be worthwhile, my research was out of date.

I had now spent two years writing two books that did not get published. Still, I didn't regret the year that I spent writing the Alzheimer's book because the knowledge I gained helped me understand and care for my father.

About that time, I went to a wedding, usually a happy event, but in this case I grew uneasy as I listened to the vows that were spoken. The bride, a lively young woman with a great sense of humor, solemnly promised to let her husband be head of the household and make all the decisions. I wondered how my friend could make such a pledge.

She had spent months planning the flowers, what the bridal party would wear, and the food for the reception, but clearly she had given no thought to the most important part of the wedding: the vows.

I wish I could have written those wedding vows for her, I thought.

I paid little attention to the rest of the ceremony, for I was mentally writing wedding vows. A book idea had just been born.

Beginning writers are often told to write about what they know best. I knew about love. I knew about a happy marriage. I knew my friend should not be agreeing to let her husband decide everything in what ought to be an equal partnership. (Less than two years later, she was divorced.)

The morning after the wedding, I called my minister. "Do many couples write their own wedding vows?" I asked.

"Lots of them want to," he replied, "but they don't know how to go about it. Usually they end up using the standard vows. Then they'll add a poem or reading to personalize the ceremony."

I called a Catholic priest, a Unitarian minister, and a justice of the peace and got the same response each time. Couples want to write their own personal vows, but they don't know how.

I checked *Books in Print*, a reference book that lists all books that are currently available, to see if there was already a resource for such couples. There wasn't, so I began writing original wedding vows, along with suggestions on how couples could use my vows as a starting point to write their own. I also wrote ring ceremonies and anniversary vows. Six months later, I had a book manuscript.

Once again I sent it to the agent who had tried to sell my novel but had returned the Alzheimer's book. She returned this manuscript, too.

"You write so well," she said, "but I have no market for this book. None of the publishers I work with have published anything like this."

This time, instead of crying over her letter, I got angry. They haven't published anything like this, I thought, because it's a new idea. Publishers always say they want fresh material, but now she can't sell it because it's *too* different.

This agent worked for a large agency and dealt with all the well-known publishing companies. If she saw no market for my book of wedding vows, I knew I had a problem.

I also knew that she wasn't the right agent for me, and I never sent her anything else.

Contemporary Drama Service, where I had published many of my plays, is a part of Meriwether Publishing, which publishes books. I submitted

Vows of Love and Marriage to Meriwether, and they decided to publish it. I still get goosebumps when I remember learning that my first book would be published.

Vows of Love and Marriage was published in 1979 and stayed in print for ten years. A paperback edition, *Wedding Vows: How to Express Your Love in Your Own Words,* is still in print.

Every writer looks forward to the day when the first copy of his or her book arrives. I had dedicated *Vows of Love and Marriage* to Carl, but he didn't know that. It began a tradition that has continued with every book: I don't tell who the book is dedicated to until the book is published. Then I give the first copy to that person.

I could hardly wait! Daily I imagined handing Carl that first copy of my first published book. He would be so excited and happy! Perhaps we would go out to dinner to celebrate, carrying a copy of the book to show to everyone we met. It would be a glorious, never-to-be-forgotten event.

Like so many things in life, it didn't quite work out as planned.

I lived in Washington, and my brother, Art, lived

in Minnesota. Throughout the sixteen years of our father's illness, Art and I both went to California, where our parents lived, several times a year.

On the day my first book arrived, I was flying to California to visit my parents. The box of books came just before I had to leave for the airport.

I opened the package, admired the cover design, checked to be sure the dedication was right, and stuck one book in my suitcase to give to my mother. I left the rest on the dining room table, where I knew Carl would find them when he got home.

Later that night, by telephone, he told me how pleased he was by the dedication. We agreed it was a wonderful book, but our enthusiasm was dampened by worries over Father's worsening mental condition. The once-in-a-lifetime moment of seeing my first book in print was not as joyful as it should have been because my father was so sick.

I have used Alzheimer's disease many times in my writing. Anything that has such a major impact on my life will find its way into my work. The first time was my play, *Spirit!* One of my favorite characters, Esther, has severe memory loss. Like my father was, she is childlike and completely unaware of her former career. That play was written before my dad forgot how to feed himself.

I also used my experience in *Night of Fear,* a novel about a boy named T.J. whose grandmother has Alzheimer's disease. T.J. is appalled by Grandma Ruth's brain disorder and embarrassed by her behavior when his friends are there. He remembers the vital, intelligent woman she was, and wishes desperately that she could be that way again.

T.J., of course, is based on me—just as all my main characters are, the boys as well as the girls. They have my thoughts and my feelings because those are the thoughts and feelings I know best.

Often in the early years of Father's disease I shed bitter tears over the enormous injustice of this vibrant and intelligent man's mental decline.

After eight years of caring for him at home, Mother was tired and too thin. Father couldn't talk or dress himself. Twice he fell and couldn't get up again. It was hard to find reliable home health care. Although it had seemed unthinkable to let strangers care for him in an unfamiliar place, it was clear that soon we would have no other choice.

I flew to California again, and Mother hired

someone to stay with Father one afternoon while we looked at nursing homes. After we returned from this sad task, I sat in the den and tried to distract myself with a magazine.

Soon Father shuffled into the den. He no longer spoke to me, but I believed that he still knew who I was. He smiled a docile, little-boy smile, and I knew he was glad to see me.

As I watched him, I remembered the piano duets we had played when I was growing up. I recalled family card games with my aunts and uncles, when Father always figured out which cards everyone else held. I thought of the many times when I'd shrieked that the swimming pool was too cold, and Father had replied, with a grin, "Just like a warm bath."

I recalled how his good humor and thoughtfulness had cheered me and my roommates when I had polio. I remembered the outgoing businessman who had invited me to the Rotary Club's annual father-daughter luncheon, and the handsome man in a tuxedo who'd walked me down the aisle on my wedding day.

Impulsively, I went to him and said, "You have been a wonderful father to me."

His eyes brimmed with tears.

I took his hands and spoke of all my special memories. Then I put my arms around him, drew him close, and whispered, "I love you." His arms tightened around me.

At that moment, I knew that I would always love him, no matter what his physical or mental condition. I loved the bright, successful, fun-loving father that I used to have, but I also loved this elderly man with his childish ways and sweet smile.

I quit raging at fate and set out to keep Father as contented and comfortable as possible.

I treasure my memory of that day, thankful that I told him how much he meant to me while he was still able to comprehend. All too soon the day came when his mind was so imprisoned by Alzheimer's disease that my words could no longer scale the walls.

❋

From the ending of *Night of Fear*:

Gently, T.J. helped her to her feet. Then he put his arms around her and held her close.

A deep love for the Grandma Ruth of his childhood filled T.J.'s heart. He had not realized until that night, when so many memories flooded over him, what an influence she had been on his life. *Wishing won't help ... win with your wits ... take action.* For the first time, he appreciated how much she had taught him, how his thinking and personality had been shaped by the person she had been. He knew he would always treasure his memories of that wonderful woman.

But this Grandma Ruth, the here-and-now Grandma Ruth, was special, too, and despite her Alzheimer's disease, he loved her, just the way she was. Never again would he waste time and energy longing for her to go back to her former self. He would quit denying the truth of her disease. He would quit wishing that she wasn't sick and take action to make her happy, if he could, because he loved this mixed-up old woman with her purse full of Monopoly money and her childlike smile, the one who thought he was David.

Tears dripped onto the keyboard as I wrote that scene, and I still cry every time I read it because it brings back the day in my parents' den when I hugged my father and spoke from my heart.

{ I O }

At Last! Books for Kids

As my writing income gradually increased and our children finished college, Carl and I decided it was his turn to follow a dream. His hobby of restoring antique musical instruments had become more and more important to him. After thirty-five years in the dairy industry, he left to start a business restoring player pianos, crank organs, and other old instruments. His new occupation resulted in my second book.

For a time, he both refinished the exterior of pianos and rebuilt their mechanical parts. The finish on the wood often crinkles with age, and many pianos had cigarette burns in the wood or stains where drinking glasses had been set. Carl removed the old finish, returning the wood to its original beauty.

Over and over, I heard people tell him that they

wanted to refinish their own pianos. "How do I do it?" they asked.

This question does not have a twenty-five-words-or-less answer. It isn't easy to refinish a piano. After enough people had asked Carl how to do it, I realized that perhaps I could write a how-to book.

I sat in Carl's workshop while he measured and mixed a batch of his own formula for stripping off the old finish. I watched him take a piano apart. This is necessary because otherwise the stripping solution drips onto the piano's internal parts.

He explained each step while I tape-recorded his comments. Then I rewrote the material in my own words, trying to say everything simply and clearly.

A friend shot some photos. I held lights, gave unnecessary advice, and served lunch. We also went to another friend's home to take color photos of his piano, which Carl had refinished.

When the book was done, I sent it to a different agent, a woman I had met at a conference.

She sold it quickly, but the terms of my contract with the publisher were terrible. Usually, a publisher agrees to pay an author royalties. This means that every time a copy of the book is sold, the author receives a percentage of the price. This contract gave me only a small one-time payment. No matter how many years the book stayed in print or how many copies it sold, I would not get any royalties.

When I balked at that, the agent told me I should feel lucky to sell the book at all.

Afraid that if I didn't sign the contract, I would have yet another unsold book in my desk drawer, I accepted the terms, and *Refinishing and Restoring Your Piano* was published.

I had called the book *How to Refinish Your Piano*, and I argued long and hard against using the word "restoring" in the title. In Carl's business, restoring means making the mechanical parts work the way they did originally, and my book did not go into that. In the end, the publishers used the title they wanted.

Despite the problems, I was happy with the book.

I had my byline on many magazine pieces and plays by then, but a book is different. A book feels substantial. A book hints of immortality. Every time I went to the library I looked up my own name and was always glad to find it, along with the titles of my books. Both of them.

About then, I received another letter that

changed my life. This one was from the editor who had published the book of wedding vows and some of my plays.

"We want to publish a book of monologs for students," he told me, "and we'd like you to write it for us."

I hesitated. Monologs are short dramatic pieces that one person reads or recites from memory. I knew that actors often used them as audition pieces, and speech and drama teachers assigned them as classroom practice, but was there really a market for such a book? On the other hand, editors were not waiting in line to buy books from me. I decided to give it a try, and I began writing monologs from a kid's point of view.

Because most monologs are only two or three pages long, I needed many different ideas in order to fill a book. I ended up with sixty-five monologs, and I loved every minute of the work.

Some of the monologs were funny, some were sad. I wrote about a first date, braces on teeth, dreams of being a professional athlete, school cafeteria lunches, fire drills, and Halloween candy. One monolog, "My Blankee," fondly recalls a special baby blanket. Another gives detailed instructions on the best way to eat cotton candy. My favorite, "The Winner," is about a girl who loses a poetry contest but gains far more than the twenty-five-dollar prize.

As I wrote, I realized that in writing for children, I had found, at last, my true voice as a writer.

I had spent ten years as a professional writer since that first unsold mystery. I knew my work had improved. When I finished *Winning Monologs for Young Actors*, I decided to write another novel, a mystery for young readers.

When my new agent heard this, she said, "Don't do it. It's next to impossible to sell a children's novel these days. Write another how-to book instead."

"I don't know enough about anything else to write a how-to book," I replied. "Besides, I want to write fiction."

"Nonfiction is easier to sell," she said.

I considered her warning. If I never write another novel, I thought, then I'll have no chance of publishing one. If I write one, at least there will be a possibility of publication. I never regret things I've written, but I knew I would regret *not* writing what I most wanted to do. I decided to take the risk.

With the agent's gloomy predictions of failure ringing in my ears, I began a new novel. This time, I paid attention to what had been published recently. I read dozens of children's books. Whenever I especially liked one, I read it again. The first time I wanted to see what happened; the second time I paid attention to how the author had handled suspense and characterization.

The idea for my novel came from Bob, who was then teaching in a junior high school. One day he arrived at school and learned that a student was missing. She had been in class the day before. Her books and coat were found in her home, and there was no sign of a struggle, but she was gone. Bob told me how upset the other students were when they learned that their classmate had disappeared.

I didn't follow the real case because I didn't want to write a true crime story, but the situation of a youngster arriving at school to learn that a friend was missing became the basis of *Deadly Stranger*.

My first novel had taken me a year to write; this one took nine months. I hoped my writing was better as well as faster.

I sent the manuscript to the agent, who was still

urging me to write another how-to book because novels for kids were impossible to sell. I then tried to forget about my story, but I couldn't let go of the characters I liked so well. Fearful of rejection, I waited. I didn't have to wait long.

Only two weeks later, the agent called. "I've sold your book!" she said.

I was so stunned that for a moment I couldn't imagine what book she meant. Surely not my novel; it was too soon. Had she called me by mistake?

"*My* book?" I said.

"The children's novel. I sent it to Dodd, Mead and they've accepted it." When I didn't respond immediately, she added, "They're a well-known New York publisher."

The news finally sank in. Although my hands shook as I wrote, I collected my wits enough to write down the terms that Dodd, Mead had offered, including the payment of royalties.

"I think you should accept this offer," the agent said.

"Yes," I said. "I'll accept it." Of course I would accept it; I would have agreed to anything. My novel was going to be published!

"This is quite an accomplishment," she said.

"I know," I replied, and I did.

As soon as I hung up, I told Carl, then called Anne, Bob, and all of my friends. The day I learned that my first novel would be published remains a high point of my life.

Like every novelist, I hoped my book would be a best-seller. Months later, when the book was actually published, my first review began with the words, "A cliff-hanger!" It was exactly what I had hoped for.

When a local bookstore offered to host a book-signing, I happily agreed. For years I had day-dreamed about sitting in a bookstore with a stack of my books on the table, signing autographs. At last, it was really going to happen.

We set a date, the store ran an ad in the newspaper, I told all my friends, and I arrived early with pen in hand.

"We have a bit of a problem," the owner said. "The books didn't get here."

My happiness drained away as if a plug had been pulled inside me. I sat at the special table in the store and chatted with customers. Carl did his best to act cheerful. I signed one book of monologs and the book of vows, which the store already had. Many friends came, and one of Carl's brothers showed up, but I had no new book to show them. My first bookstore event was not at all the way I had hoped it would be.

Shortly after *Deadly Stranger* was released, the publisher, which had published books for one hundred years, went out of business. The editor who had bought *Deadly Stranger,* and to whom I had just sent the manuscript of my next book, *Nightmare Mountain,* was now out of a job.

Even with no publisher and no editor, my future was clear to me. From the minute *Deadly Stranger* was accepted, I never wrote anything for adults. Writing for kids was way more fun.

The Ideas Box

When I talk about my books to children, they usually ask, "Where do you get your ideas?" The way I wrote *Nightmare Mountain* is typical.

On my desk, I have what I call my Ideas Box. This contains many odd bits of information. Sometimes Carl and I will go out to dinner, and when he starts to say something to me, I'll put my finger to my lips and whisper, "Shhh." I'm listening to what the people at the next table are talking about, and it's giving me a story idea. I'll scribble that on a slip of paper, and when we get home, it goes into my Ideas Box.

One summer we went to the county fair where

there was an exhibit of llamas. Being an animal lover, I petted a llama and talked with its owner.

The next day, I went to the library and checked out everything I could find about llamas. As I read, I made notes on 3 x 5 cards. I put a rubber band around the notes and put them into my Ideas Box.

Later that summer, there was an avalanche on Mount Baker in Washington State. Two hikers were buried under the snow and weren't rescued until the next day. When I read this in the newspaper, I thought how scary it would be to get caught in an avalanche. I clipped out the newspaper article and put it in my Ideas Box.

I kept thinking about those hikers. If they were buried under the snow, how would they know which way to dig to get to the surface? After tumbling down the mountain in an avalanche, they'd be disoriented and couldn't tell up from down. If they dug in the wrong direction, they could use up their small pocket of air.

I went back to the library and researched how to survive in the snow. I learned that if you are ever buried in the snow and don't know which way to dig to reach air, you should spit. Gravity will always pull your saliva down; then you can dig in the right direction. I added this useful tidbit to my Ideas Box.

After I sold *Deadly Stranger,* I was trying to figure out what to write next. One day I rummaged through all the material in my Ideas Box and took out three things. First, the notes about llamas. I decided to set my story on a llama ranch, and use the animals in the plot. By then I knew that llamas are expensive; I could have a llama thief as my villain.

Next out of my box was the newspaper clipping about the avalanche. What if my llama ranch sat at the foot of a mountain? My characters could climb partway up and get caught in an avalanche. It would be an exciting scene, and I could use that business about spitting, which I found fascinating.

The third item from the box was a newspaper article about a boy who was allergic to peanuts. He went to a birthday party, ate a cookie that had ground-up peanuts in it, went into a coma, and died.

I used all three of those items in *Nightmare Mountain,* though my character recovers from the coma instead of dying. The whole book grew from things I found interesting: the llamas at the fair, the avalanche, and the peanut allergy.

Because llamas are such handsome animals, I assumed a llama would be featured on the cover, but there have been four editions of *Nightmare Mountain* over the years, including one in Danish, and not one of them shows a llama.

Although I never got a llama on a book cover, students in Indiana built a life-size llama out of paper-mâché the week before I visited their school, and a school in Arizona gave me a special surprise. When I arrived to talk to the students, four live llamas greeted me in the schoolyard! They made me think of the "Mary Had a Little Lamb" nursery rhyme, with a slight change: it made the author laugh and play, to see a llama at school.

Some book ideas grew from my own childhood. I used to make believe I could fly. I held my arms out like airplane wings while I ran around my yard, eyes closed, pretending to swoop over faraway places. Then I "landed" in a made-up country and imagined that I was exploring it.

Years later, my flying game was the origin of the Instant Commuter, a device used to travel through time and space. Warren and Betsy, the characters in

logy," use the Instant Commuter to
ption of Mount Saint Helens in 1980
State, the Armistice Day blizzard
he Midwest, and the Johnstown,
lood in 1889.

Many readers have let me know that they wished
they had such a machine. One boy wrote to ask me,
"If you really had an Instant Commuter, where
would you go?"

I told him I would travel back in time to when my
parents were alive and well, and spend a day with
them again. Where you go is less important than who
you're with.

Some ideas sit in my Ideas Box for years and
never become books. Other ideas send me straight
to the computer, full of enthusiasm, the minute I get
them.

Sometimes an idea changes so much as I write
that the finished book has little in common with the
idea that got me started. I began a story set in Africa,
about an American boy and an African boy who dis-
agreed over elephant poaching. I ended up with
The Hideout, which is set in the Pacific Northwest
and is about a boy who tries to hide from his

troubles and instead has even more trouble with a bear poacher.

Why did I revise my plot? First, I learned from my research that laws about the sale of ivory (the reason for elephant poaching) keep changing, and I didn't want my book to be out of date. Second, I learned that bear poaching is a big problem in North America. Poachers even kill bears within our national parks! I hadn't known that before. My new knowledge made me angry and changed my story.

I like to experiment with different kinds of writing. Besides mysteries, I've written adventure, humor, time-travel, and realistic problem novels. I did a second book of monologs and a book of monologs, dialogs, and short playlets called *Acting Natural.* I wrote one series and one book of true dog stories. Two books have a cat as my co-author!

One day when I wasn't home, Carl answered the phone. "This is the Library of Congress calling," he was told. "I need to speak with Peg Kehret."

Carl said I wasn't there, identified himself, and asked if he could help. The Library of Congress, in Washington, D.C., is our nation's official library, and it contains a copy of every book published in America. He figured this call was important.

The caller explained, "We have many kinds of material written by people named Peg Kehret. We want to find out which of these your wife wrote and which were written by a different Peg Kehret."

Carl said, "There's another Peg Kehret who is a writer?"

"Oh, yes. We have a wide variety of work under that name."

Carl knew I would be unhappy with this news as we had never heard of another Peg Kehret, much less one who was a writer. Kehret isn't exactly a common last name.

Carl said he knew everything I had written, so the caller said she would read the list of titles and Carl could say if they were mine or not.

"*Sports Skit Kit.*"

"Yes, that's hers."

"*Vows of Love and Marriage.*"

"She wrote that."

"*Winning Monologs for Young Actors.*"

"That's hers."

"*Comedy Duets?*"

"Yes."

"Did she write *Deadly Stranger?*"

"She did."

"But that's a novel," the woman said. "Those other titles were all nonfiction."

"She does both," Carl said.

"What about a play called *Dracula, Darling?*"

"Yes. She's published several plays."

It went on like that, through my other titles, with Carl saying each time that I was the author. Finally the caller said, in a tone that implied, I'll bet she didn't write *this* one, "What about *Refinishing and Restoring Your Piano?*"

"It's hers, too," Carl said.

There was a pause. "She wrote my whole list," the woman said. "There's only one Peg Kehret!"

"I'm glad to hear that," Carl said.

So was I.

Children often ask me if a particular story is true. "Did it really happen to you?" they wonder.

If everything I've written about had actually happened to me, I'd be in no condition to write this or any other book. I've never survived an avalanche or been shipwrecked off the coast of Africa or been abducted by a deranged arsonist. I haven't traveled back in time or seen a ghost or been arrested for shoplifting. I *have* experienced the emotions that each of those situations creates. I've been afraid. I've been cold, and lonely, and angry.

It is the feelings that give a novel its authenticity. When I'm able to give a character strong, true feelings—the same feelings I've experienced in other circumstances—then those characters seem real, and readers who identify with those characters will feel the emotions that I felt as I wrote.

One day I sat alone at my desk, remembering my fear when an earthquake once rocked a tall building that I was in. I wrote about Jonathan and Abby, two children alone in a campground when an earthquake strikes.

Abby is dependent on a walker, so I thought back to my recovery from polio, when I needed walking sticks in order to walk by myself. Each time I sat down I made sure my sticks were within easy reach, and I panicked if some well-meaning person put them "out of the way" where I couldn't retrieve them.

What if I still needed walking sticks, I thought, but they got destroyed in an earthquake? My feelings became Abby's helpless dread as her walker gets crushed by a fallen tree.

It's quite astonishing, when you think about it. My own remembered fear became letters on my computer screen, and those letters changed into printed words on the pages of a book.

Many months—even years—later, readers in other parts of the world can read those words and feel exactly what I felt as I wrote them. The anxiety they have for Jonathan and Abby is real.

Through the miracles of writing and reading, my deepest emotions are shared with people I have never met. Children who were not yet born when I wrote *Earthquake Terror* now tell me it is their favorite book.

{ 12 }

Helping the Animals

I've volunteered at the humane society for more than twenty-five years. My jobs have included taking puppies to visit nursing homes, petting and playing with cats so that they would get used to people, stuffing envelopes, selling cookies at the annual Adoptathon, exercising dogs, and more.

I was once a "dirty dog driver." When particularly stinky, filthy dogs were ready to be put up for adoption, volunteers drove them to a groomer to be bathed and clipped. Then the dogs were driven back to the shelter, with their chances of being chosen much improved. This duty never improved the smell of my car, though.

For five years, I wrote a "Pet of the Month" feature for a small newspaper. I usually chose an older animal who was not as likely to get adopted as a cute little puppy or kitten. I drove the animal to a community center where I met a photographer. She would shoot some pictures, and I would give her the article I'd written.

Usually I took dogs because they were easier to transport; they don't get as nervous as cats do. The first time I took a cat, he got so upset on the way home that he threw up. This didn't help the smell of my car, either.

When a new photographer, Greg Farrar, was hired, he offered to come to the humane society so the animals wouldn't have to travel. After that I often wrote about cats as well as dogs, and once my Pet of the Month was a rabbit.

Over and over, the pets I chose to write about were there "because the owner was moving and couldn't take the dog along." I wondered why not. Carl and I moved a lot, and we always took our animals with us. Another common reason was, "My landlord doesn't allow pets." (So, live somewhere else, I thought.) The worst reason of all was, "I don't have time for a dog." I wanted to yell, "Then why did you get a dog in the first place?"

There are legitimate reasons why people must give up their pets, and I was glad that at least these animals were brought to a shelter rather than abandoned on the side of the road. Still, it was frustrating to see so many healthy, loving creatures in need of homes.

One dog had been dumped at a freeway rest stop. His owners simply drove off and left him behind. When I wrote a heart-wrenching account of the deserted dog for a Pet of the Month article, he got adopted the day the article was published.

My outrage at the inhumane treatment of animals never lessened, and I was glad I could help a few of them find good homes. Greg's expert photos helped, too.

My purpose with those articles was to entice people who wanted a pet to come to the humane society. Often they came to the shelter because of my monthly article but ended up adopting a different animal than the one I had written about. That was fine with me.

Greg and I had to stop the Pet of the Month feature when the newspaper quit giving the humane society free space. Years later, we worked together again when Greg took the photos for my book *Shelter Dogs: Amazing Stories of Adopted Strays.*

When I began writing for children, I knew that I wanted to use my humane society experiences in a book, but I didn't have an idea that seemed right.

Then I got myself in trouble.

In 1989, I spoke at the Pacific Northwest Writers' Conference, and as I drove home I thought how much fun it had been to spend time with other writers. I remembered when I was a nervous beginner who got lost trying to find the panel on marketing. Now I was one of the conference speakers. Unbelievable!

I drove along thinking about writing and not thinking about my driving—until I saw red lights flashing in my rear-view mirror. I pulled over and got my first (and only) speeding ticket.

"I've never had a ticket before," I told the officer. "Never?"

"Not even a parking ticket."

"Then you should go to court," he advised. "If you just pay the fine, this will cost you seventy-nine dollars, but if you go to court and the judge sees that you've never had a ticket, he'll cut the fine way down."

I thought it might be interesting to go to court, so I signed up to do that and was given a date to appear.

The large courtroom contained wooden benches filled with people awaiting their turn to talk to the judge. A clerk called out the names one at a time.

I sat down and listened for my name to be called.

Soon two obnoxious boys, both about sixteen, came in. They talked loudly, they were rude to the clerk, and every sentence they spoke contained a swear word. They made a big commotion as they arrived, and they decided to sit right next to me.

For a while they made fun of the court system. Then they began to talk and laugh about things their friends had done—terrible things that were wrong, but these boys thought they were funny.

The more they talked, the more angry I became. Finally I took a pencil and a small notebook out of my purse and I wrote down everything they said. You boys, I thought, are going to be in a book someday. I wasn't sure how or where I would use them, but they made me so furious that I knew I had to write about them. Anything that produces strong emotion in me, good or bad, goes into my work.

The boys paid no attention to my scribbling. They just kept talking while I recorded every word.

When it was my turn to talk to the judge, he could tell from his computer that I had never had a traffic violation before.

"You can either pay a forty-dollar fine," he told me, "or you can do twenty hours of community service for a nonprofit organization. If you do the community service, and if you don't get another ticket for three years, this will go off your record entirely."

I chose to do the community service. He handed me a list of nonprofit organizations where I could volunteer. I glanced at the sheet of paper; there on the list was the humane society.

This is the book I'll write, I thought. It'll be about a young person who is basically a good kid but who makes a mistake, breaks a law, goes through the juvenile court system, and is assigned to do community service work at the humane society. I knew I could use all the experiences I've had as a volunteer.

The judge must have wondered why I was smiling happily at his list. He didn't know I had the whole plot of a new book. Usually I work harder than that for a plot.

The book I wrote was *Cages*. No one gets a speeding ticket in it. Instead, it's about a girl who's caught shoplifting and is assigned to do community service at the humane society.

I didn't do my community service at the humane society because I already volunteered there. Public schools were also on the judge's list, so I fulfilled my obligation by doing author visits at schools without charging my usual fee.

There is a scene in *Cages* where the main character, Kit, is waiting outside the juvenile court committee room. Two obnoxious boys arrive and sit beside her. These were easy pages for me to write. I got out my notes from my day in court, and all I had to do was clean up the language.

One sixth-grade girl confided to me that she used

to shoplift all the time, but after she read *Cages* she decided not to do it anymore.

After reading *Cages*, many school groups have collected pet food and supplies for their local animal shelters. Dozens of young people have volunteered to help the animals. Such results are the best reward a writer can have.

Part of my royalties from each book are donated to animal welfare groups. Money from *Don't Tell Anyone* helps pay for a mobile spay/neuter clinic that prevents the births of thousands of unwanted puppies and kittens. Money from *Shelter Dogs* bought portable bathing stations so that dogs can get shampooed right at the humane society. No more dirty dog drivers!

My love of animals is one of my strongest ties to young readers because most of them love animals, too. Their letters ask about my dog and cat more often than they inquire about my husband and children.

Over and over in my books, I show the human-animal bond, which I believe is one of the most worthwhile relationships we can have. We can learn much from animals about loyalty, patience, and unconditional love. Animals don't care how we dress, or how much we weigh, or whether we're pretty or plain. They judge us only by the look of kindness in our eyes.

I wrote about elephants in *Terror at the Zoo* and *Saving Lilly*, chimpanzees in *The Secret Journey*, and llamas in *Nightmare Mountain*. I shared my outrage over poaching in *The Hideout* and *Screaming Eagles*.

My heroes and heroines love cats in *My Brother Made Me Do It, Don't Tell Anyone, Searching for Candlestick Park, The Stranger Next Door*, and *Spy Cat*. They love dogs in *Earthquake Terror, Shelter Dogs, Cages, Nightmare Mountain, The Richest Kids in Town, Sisters, Long Ago, Deadly Stranger*, and the three "disaster" books: *The Volcano Disaster, The Blizzard Disaster*, and *The Flood Disaster*.

The heroine of *I'm Not Who You Think I Am* loves her house rabbit. In *Night of Fear*, T.J. risks his own life to save a pony from a burning shed. The kids in the Frightmares books start a club to help all animals.

When I look at this list of books that show children loving an animal, I realize that every single one of my middle-grade novels is included!

I did not set out to write dozens of books about kids who love animals. It just happened. My characters love animals because I do, and I want my readers to care about animals, too. Being kind to animals can be the first step toward feeling empathy for other people.

{ 13 }

Polio Returns

In order to graduate from high school, I was required to take physical education. To pass the course, I had to do three push-ups. I couldn't do them. Every time I tried, I failed because my arm muscles weren't strong enough.

When I look back at this situation, I wonder why I didn't simply explain to my PE teacher that because I had polio when I was twelve, I couldn't do three push-ups. My muscles weren't merely weak; many of them no longer functioned at all.

I could easily have gotten a letter from my doctor, too, but instead I asked my gym partner to lie for me. She signed the paper saying I had done the three push-ups when I hadn't done even one.

The PE incident shows how my family and I felt

about my polio disabilities. My parents wanted me to be fully recovered, and so did I, so we pretended I had no permanent problems.

After I was able to walk without walking sticks, I looked completely normal. No one meeting me would have guessed I had been paralyzed from the neck down. They wouldn't know that some of my muscles had been permanently damaged, leaving me with weaknesses that could never be overcome.

I never discussed my polio experience or my lingering physical problems with any of my friends. Everyone around me acted as if I had no disability, and I never mentioned the problems that polio had created. Since I was treated like everyone else, it was easy to pretend that I was just like everyone else. At least it was easy until I tried to do three push-ups.

Perhaps this was good; perhaps not. I never used polio as an excuse not to do something, but by ignoring my physical difficulties, and by not talking about my life-changing experience, I acted as if this significant part of my life didn't matter.

My problems were more annoying than severe. I played piano, but I couldn't hold down the sustain pedal because the muscles that would have allowed me to keep my heel on the floor while I raised the ball of my foot no longer worked.

I couldn't use my diaphragm to breathe; I used my stomach muscles instead—a problem only when the high school chorus director tried to help me improve my singing. "Fill up with air!" he would exclaim. "Expand your chest!" When I tried to expand my chest, my stomach expanded instead.

I've always been round-shouldered because some of the muscles necessary to hold my shoulders back were paralyzed. My home economics teacher demanded perfect posture from her students. Every day she told me, "Put your shoulders back and stand up straight." I never explained why I kept my shoulders back for only a few seconds.

I couldn't hit a golf ball very far, or a baseball, because my arms weren't strong enough. I didn't swim well, either. Instead of acknowledging the real reason why I was so poor at sports, I said I didn't like them. "I'd rather watch baseball than play," I declared.

When I was in my fifties, I began having muscle pain, and the weakness that I'd always had in my arms and legs became worse. My toes often cramped, and I tired easily. When I read that many polio survivors were experiencing similar problems, I was shocked. Had my polio returned?

A group of doctors held a public meeting in Seattle to discuss the newly recognized "post-polio syndrome." I went to that meeting.

Before it began, I talked with people in the audience about their experiences with hot packs, wheelchairs, and separation from their families. I felt a connection with these men and women whom I had never met before. As we spoke, I felt a great relief that I could finally talk about my polio ordeal.

Discouragement soon replaced the relief. The doctors told us that there is no treatment for post-polio syndrome. No miracle drug. No therapy that would put lost strength back into my limbs. The outlook, in fact, was bleak. I might continue to lose muscle strength until I could no longer walk unaided. One of the doctors, himself a polio survivor, said many post-polio patients have had to return to the wheelchairs they gave up so many years ago.

From age thirteen on, I had drawn confidence from knowing that I had survived a terrible disease. I believed that because I had beaten polio,

I could do anything else I chose to do in life.

I had not conquered polio, after all. Later that month, a medical exam confirmed what I feared: post-polio syndrome was causing my weakness, pain, and fatigue.

I prepared for a rematch. This time, it would be a different kind of battle. I couldn't defeat post-polio syndrome, but I could control how I reacted to it.

It was time to tell my own story.

I began to write about my polio experience, to put into words what had happened to me all those years ago that I had never talked about.

Each morning I went to my desk and dredged up the memories. I remembered my hospital room-mates, my doctors and nurses, my physical therapists. I laughed as I wrote, and I cried. My tears were for that long-ago girl who endured so much, and also because I yearned to have my father back, and my grandpa, and B.J.

For the first time, I wrote about the pain and the fear. The recollections poured forth as a psychological dam, built long ago, finally crumbled in my mind.

The first three publishers who read my book

Small Steps: The Year I Got Polio turned it down. They didn't think kids would be interested in polio because it's no longer a threat to them.

I thought this was just a polite way to say no, that my book really wasn't good enough to get published.

If I had been submitting *Small Steps* on my own, I would have put it away after the first publisher decided against it, and it would have ended up unsold in my desk drawer along with my first novel and the book about Alzheimer's disease. But by then I had an agent whose tastes matched mine. Luckily, she was not so easily discouraged. Each time a publisher declined *Small Steps*, my agent said, "Their loss," and sent it out again.

When Albert Whitman & Company agreed to publish *Small Steps*, my joy surpassed even the delight I'd felt at the acceptance of my first novel. This book was personal; it meant more to me than anything else I had ever written.

The publisher wanted to put a picture of me in my wheelchair on the cover. I looked through all the old family photos and found none of me sitting in the wheelchair.

I called my mother, who told me that after I could

walk on my own, she had destroyed every photo of me in my wheelchair and every picture of me using my walking sticks.

"I didn't want to remember you that way," she explained. "I wanted to put polio behind us."

Her action reflected society's attitude at that time. In 1950, a person who couldn't walk was considered "crippled." It was thought that such people could never lead as full a life or contribute as much as those without a handicap. President Franklin D. Roosevelt, who was also a polio survivor, hid his disability from the public, too, and his was harder to conceal than mine.

With my consent, the publisher put a picture of Dorothy and Alice, two of my hospital roommates, on the cover of *Small Steps.* This decision caused no end of confusion. Readers assumed, quite naturally, that since my book was a memoir, I was in the cover picture. Dozens of readers asked, "Which one is Peg?"

When the paperback edition was being planned, the publishers and I agreed that my picture should be on the cover, even without my wheelchair. A photo of me that had originally been in the middle of the book was exchanged with the picture of Alice and Dorothy.

When *Small Steps* came out, even people who knew me well were surprised to learn that I'd had polio.

For three years in high school, my friend Margaret and I spent as much time as possible together. We slept at each other's homes, sang duets, went to basketball games, and shared our innermost thoughts. After graduation, we kept in touch.

When Margaret read *Small Steps*, she called me. "You never told me about having polio!" she said. "In high school, I thought I knew every detail of your life, but I never knew about your most extraordinary experience. I can't believe it!"

I can't believe it myself. My only explanation is that my parents chose to "put polio behind us." Because they never talked about my hospital experiences, I didn't talk about them, either.

Of all my books, *Small Steps* was the hardest to write, partly because I had to tell the truth. When I write fiction, if something doesn't work well in the story, I change it. I make up characters and motivation and events. *Small Steps* is about real people.

It's more difficult to be honest about my own thoughts and feelings than about those of imagined characters.

In my case, the truth was liberating. Telling my own story helped me accept my past and made it easier for me to deal with my ongoing polio problems. If a young girl could survive such an experience and be emotionally stronger for it, then surely a mature woman can live with some physical problems and be emotionally and spiritually stronger, too. I've been far more fortunate than many polio survivors. I've had over fifty years of nearly normal mobility, and I'm grateful for those years.

After *Small Steps* was published, I got hundreds of letters from readers. One of my favorites was from a mother who told me her son began weeping at the end of the book. When she asked why he was crying, he said, "Because the best book I'll ever read is over."

Many children wrote to me about the physical problems they faced. I heard from kids with multiple sclerosis, diabetes, broken bones, muscular dystrophy—even one child who described, in bloody detail, her cut finger.

As the mail from kids with physical problems poured in, I decided to write a book about a disease that some of them still have to battle, the way I fought to overcome polio. Once again, I started reading medical material. I considered lupus and cancer in addition to the diseases already mentioned.

In the end, I chose juvenile rheumatoid arthritis (JRA). I had read that two hundred thousand kids in the U.S. have this disease. My immediate reaction was that most children would detest that diagnosis because they think arthritis is a problem for old people. Grandparents have arthritis, not kids.

As I read about the problems that JRA causes, I was reminded of my own struggle with polio. I knew I could write convincingly about this disease.

My Brother Made Me Do It is written entirely in letters from Julie, who has JRA, to her eighty-nine-year-old pen pal, Mrs. Kaplan.

The character of Mrs. Kaplan is based on my mother. She sees the good in every situation, she invents marvelous stories, she is loyal to friends and family, and she accepts what life hands her with humor and grace.

I liked Mrs. Kaplan so much, and she became so

real to me, that I wept when I wrote of her death. Yet that character still lives because of my book, just as my parents live on in the minds of those who read *Small Steps.*

Perhaps I don't write books for my readers so much as I write them for myself.

{ 14 }

Research and Revision

Although I write mostly fiction, I can't just make up everything out of my head. I still need to do research. Some books require more research than others, but I've had to do some investigation for every book.

I especially enjoyed the research for *Searching for Candlestick Park*. While I was writing that book, Carl and I flew to San Francisco and attended a Giants' baseball game.

Before the game started, I interviewed one of the ushers. He explained his duties and told me about all the items people have left behind when they leave the stadium. Much of what he said is included in the book.

As I sat in the stands, I wrote a description of the day, the crowd, even the small airplane trailing an advertising banner.

I went to San Francisco's Greyhound Bus station, too, and I walked the streets where my character, Spencer, walks so that when I wrote those scenes, I could do it accurately. I did the same thing in Seattle, where Spencer's journey began.

I took pictures of the ballpark in San Francisco, which at that time was 3Com Park. I sent those to my editor, to be forwarded to the artist. In case he used the ballpark in the cover art, I wanted it to look right.

Unfortunately, that was the only time my research included a trip to California to see a ball game. Most research is done by reading reference books, making phone calls, searching the Internet, or interviewing people.

The Secret Journey is about a girl in 1834 who sneaks aboard a sailing ship, hoping to accompany her parents to France. Instead, she gets on a notorious slave ship bound for Africa. Here are some of the things I needed to find out while I was writing *The Secret Journey*.

1. What foods would be served in Liverpool, England, in 1834? 2. What coin might a sailor there give to a boy who helps him? 3. What did the waterfront area look like? 4. What were sailing ships like at that time? 5. What constellations are visible from the deck of a ship off the coast of Africa in June? 6. What is the temperature of the ocean at that time and place? 7. How do chimpanzees behave? 8. What are the symptoms of malaria?

I like doing research, and I strive for accuracy. Sometimes I need to ask an expert for help. I found out the ocean temperature for *The Secret Journey* by calling a friend who works for the National Oceanic and Atmospheric Administration (NOAA), and I got the correct constellations from an astronomy professor at the University of Washington.

Sometimes I ask an expert to read an entire manuscript before I send it to my publisher. *The Volcano Disaster* was read by the lead interpreter at the Mount Saint Helens Visitor Center, and *Terror at the Zoo* was read by two people in the education department at Seattle's Woodland Park Zoo.

One of the Woodland Park readers told me, "We like the book, but you made a mistake. You mentioned a kangaroo, and we have no kangaroos in this zoo."

"Then what are those animals with pouches and big tails, that hop along on their hind legs?" I asked.

"They're wallaroos," I was told. "It's a kind of kangaroo."

Before I submitted the manuscript, I changed it to say wallaroo.

Then I heard from my editor. "What in the world is a wallaroo?" she asked. "No one will know what you're talking about. Can't you just say kangaroo?"

Well, no, I couldn't. Not after the zoo people had objected.

I changed the sentence again, this time saying, "wallaroo, a kind of kangaroo," and I hoped everyone was happy with that.

Except for the unpublished book about Alzheimer's disease, the most time I ever spent researching one book was for *Shelter Dogs: Amazing Stories of Adopted Strays.* Each of the eight chapters in the book required one or more interviews with the dog's owner.

But first I had to find the right combination of dogs for the book. This took days of phone calls before I ever began the interviews.

For example, I wanted to include a dog who had rescued his family from a fire, so I called the non-emergency number for every fire department in the Puget Sound region, where I live. I left messages explaining who I was, the kind of book I was writing, and what I was looking for. "If you know of a dog who rescued someone from a fire," I concluded, "please call me."

Someone from the Redmond, Washington, fire department called back to tell me about Ivan, a dog who had rescued a mother and child from their burning home. Both people were hearing-impaired and couldn't hear the fire alarm.

My first question was, "Do you know where they got Ivan?" Since the focus of my book was dogs who came from animal shelters, I couldn't use the fire story, no matter how compelling it was, if the dog had been purchased from a breeder or pet shop.

The fire department spokesman didn't know Ivan's background, but when I tracked down the dog's owner, I learned that she had adopted Ivan from the county animal shelter. Ivan's owner didn't hear well enough to talk to me on the telephone so I interviewed her via e-mail.

I've had to find out the cost of a license to pilot a hot air balloon and the black market price for a bear's gall bladder.

I've stood on the bank of a river where bald eagles go to catch salmon. I've examined (carefully!) antique Wedgwood china, attended a cat show, and had myself hypnotized. I once checked out so many library books about poisons that the librarian asked me to show identification.

Many times the research never shows in the manuscript. For two books, *Deadly Stranger* and *I'm Not Who You Think I Am*, I had to learn about mental illness, to be sure that the characters behaved in ways that were consistent with their sickness.

I also do extensive revision on every book. By now it would seem I should be able to write a flawless first draft. So far that hasn't happened. I usually write every book at least four times before I'm satisfied.

I rewrote the first sentence of *Saving Lilly* twenty-two times. The final version goes like this: "Not many sixth-graders get an opportunity to save an elephant."

I work on a computer and do most of the revision that way. When the book seems as good as I can make it, I print it out. As soon as I read the words on paper, I see many places in need of revision. I go through the manuscript, making corrections in pencil. Then I put those changes on the computer and print again.

When I think the manuscript is finished, I send it to my editor, whose job is to be sure the writing is clear, interesting, and has no errors. Sometimes I'm asked to add material, or cut part of what I've written. It isn't easy to eliminate paragraphs or even whole pages that I've labored over. Most of the time I take the editor's advice, but not always.

The editors don't tell me how to make the changes. They note what needs to be fixed, but it's up to me to do the repairs.

A few times I have been asked to change the book's title. When I wrote a book called *What Happened to Grandma Ruth?* my editor wisely pointed out that my title probably wouldn't appeal to my readers. That book became *Night of Fear.*

First drafts are plain hard work for me, partly because I don't outline in advance. I just jump into the story with a vague idea of the plot. Usually I don't know how it will end until I write the ending.

Revisions are my favorite part of the writing process. I especially like to play with words, to see if I can improve a description or add color or texture to a scene. In my first drafts, I usually tell what the characters see and hear as well as how they feel. Later revisions often include what the characters taste, smell, or touch.

In *Don't Tell Anyone*, Megan hides from her kidnapper in the forest. The first draft said, "She came to a large fir tree and hid behind it." In the final version, I added, "She pressed herself against the rough bark. The tree smelled like Christmastime; Megan blinked back tears as she thought of Mom and Kylie."

Toward the end of my revising, I read through the manuscript once, trying to cut three words from each page. This process tightens the story, and those excess words aren't missed.

A student once confronted me after a school talk and said, "My teacher paid you to say that, didn't she?"

"To say what?" I asked.

"That part about rewriting your books. She paid you to say that, didn't she?"

I assured her that no teacher had bribed me to include anything in my talk, but I could tell she didn't believe me.

Later she and her teacher came to the table where I was signing books.

"Lesley thinks I paid you to say you revise your work," the teacher said. By the twinkle in her eyes, I knew she must have been telling Lesley all year about the importance of revision.

I held up my right hand. "I swear she didn't ask me to say that," I said.

The teacher held up her right hand. "I swear I didn't even meet Peg until after her talk."

Lesley looked at us, sighed loudly, and walked away.

"Thank you," the teacher whispered. "Lesley wants to be a writer, and she has talent, but she won't revise her work."

If she wants to be a writer, I thought, she had better revise her attitude.

{ 15 }

Talk, Talk, Talk

S oon after *Deadly Stranger* was published, I was invited to speak to the Honors English class at a middle school. I agreed to do it, and then panicked. What would I say? I was a writer, not a public speaker.

I called a writer friend who visits dozens of schools each year and asked her advice.

"Oh, just tell them how you wrote your book," she said. "Say where you got your idea, and answer their questions. It's easy."

I wasn't so sure about that. I'm frequently ill at ease with people. Except with family and close friends, I often feel awkward, as if I am there by mistake. How was I going to talk to an entire class?

I considered calling the school back and inventing an excuse not to come.

Instead I spent several days making notes and hoping I would not be too boring.

When the day came, I arrived early. The teacher greeted me, said she had a quick errand to do before class started, and left.

I was alone in the room when the bell rang. As the students filed in, I smiled at them nervously.

Two boys came in together. One whispered to the other, "Rats. We have a sub today."

"That isn't a sub," the second boy said. "That's the author!"

The first boy looked me over. "That's the author?" he said, clearly astonished. "She looks like someone you'd see in the grocery store."

He was right, and at that moment, I would have felt far more at ease pushing my cart through the produce aisle at Safeway.

I don't remember exactly what I talked about that day, but the students seemed interested, asked lots of questions, and the teacher was grateful that I had come. I was mostly relieved to have it over.

This was the first of several hundred school

visits. As I published more books for kids, and my books became better known, many speaking invitations came in. I visited nearly all of my local schools and found it was fun to meet my readers. Such visits also sold a lot of books, which kept my publishers happy.

Before long I was asked to talk at schools in other states, usually for several days at a time. I went whenever I could work the invitation into my schedule.

I quickly grew tired of flying off alone and staying by myself in hotels, so Carl and I bought a small motor home, got the license plate BKS4KDS, and began traveling together to do book talks. We took our dog, Daisy, and our cat, Pete, with us.

On our first motor home trip, I talked at twenty-six schools and two public libraries, spoke to ten groups at a children's literature festival, and autographed books at two bookstores.

We were busy, but we loved traveling by motor home.

One weekend, we stayed at the Indiana Dunes National Recreation Area. It rained Saturday night, and when we got up the next morning we found a tiny kitten hiding under our motor home, trying to stay dry. There were only a few other campsites occupied. We carried the kitten to each of them, but none of the campers had lost her.

We spoke to the park ranger who told us, "People drop off unwanted kittens here all the time. Usually the coyotes eat them, or they get run over."

A car had parked for a time in the campsite across from us the night before, but the people had left without spending the night. Had they come only to abandon an unwanted kitten?

The idea that anyone would be so cowardly and inhumane made me furious. I cuddled the kitten in my arms.

"Pretty smart cat," Carl remarked. "A big campground like this, and she found the humane society volunteers."

We were concerned that the kitten might have a disease that Pete or Daisy would catch, and we didn't need another animal in the motor home. Still, we couldn't just leave her at the campground.

"Maybe there's a humane society near here," I suggested. "They could find a good home for such a pretty kitten."

We drove to the local animal shelter. It was under-staffed, overflowing with animals, and struggling financially. Someone examined the kitten, then said she appeared to be healthy and they would take her. But it was clear to us that they had too many cats already. Instead of leaving the kitten for them to worry about, we gave them a donation and took the kitten with us.

The next morning, Carl dropped me off at the school where I was to talk. While I spoke to the students, he found a veterinarian who examined the kitten, pronounced her in good health, wormed her, and gave her the first set of vaccinations.

We named her Molly, after the heroine in *Nightmare Mountain.*

We quickly learned that two cats in a motor home are far different from one. They slept all day, then put on what came to be known as the Cat Follies between two and three o'clock each morning. They galloped back and forth, jumped from bed to couch to floor, wrestled with each other, leaped over Daisy (which made her bark), shredded the toilet paper, and generally kept us awake.

Each night during the Cat Follies, we told each

other that as soon as we got home we would take Molly to the humane society where we volunteer and put her up for adoption. We never did, though. By the time we got back home we were too fond of her to give her up.

Naturally, a book came out of this experience. *Desert Danger,* the fourth book in my Frightmares series, is about two girls on a camping trip who find an abandoned kitten in the campground.

During the next few years, we made a fall trip and a spring trip every year, traveling to a different part of the country each time. One advantage of motor home travel was that I went to schools in small towns, far from major airports. Often I was the first author ever to visit.

Along with the small schools, I spoke at large conferences of teachers and librarians. My stomach churned before such speeches. I always spent a lot of time deciding what I would say and then I practiced saying it, clocking myself to be sure I was within the time frame I'd been given. Daisy is an excellent audience when I'm practicing a speech. She listens politely, never interrupts, and only rarely falls asleep while I'm talking.

No matter how well prepared I was, the jitters always got me. Sometimes my knees shook so much that I had to hold on to the podium for fear my legs would buckle. I usually printed out my talk, but then my hands shook so hard the pages rattled when I turned them.

What finally saved me from being so scared was the audiences. They always listened intently, and afterward many people came up to thank me or to say my remarks were just what they needed to hear. Their kind words meant more than they will ever know.

The year after my mother died, I mentioned her death in a speech to the Texas Library Association. As soon as I spoke the words, a wave of grief washed over me, and I was unable to continue my talk. I stood there in front of several hundred people, struggling to control my tears, feeling foolish and apologetic. Then, from every corner of the room, spontaneous applause broke out. People clapped, letting me know they understood, and that my tears were okay.

I still have a few butterflies before a major speech, but now as soon as I'm introduced, I look out at the smiling faces and I know I have nothing to worry about. These people are not just an audience—they are my friends.

I look forward to signing books after my talks. I like the chance to visit with my readers, and after all those years of "dejection slips," it is amazing to see a long line of people waiting for me to autograph their books.

I was asked to talk to kids in Seattle's juvenile detention center. When I arrived, I went through a metal detector, then through a locked door which was watched by an armed guard.

My destination was a small room that served as a library. An earnest young librarian who wanted to make a difference in the lives of her patrons waited for me. She had placed some of my books on a table.

"After you speak, they can check out books if they want to," she said.

Soon my audience arrived: twelve teenage boys, all wearing orange jumpsuits and identical bored expressions. As they filed in, they barely glanced at me. Their body language clearly said, "You have nothing to say that will interest us."

I suspected they were right.

The chairs formed a circle. Each boy sat down, leaned his head on the back of the chair, stretched his legs out in front of him, and closed his eyes.

I knew I could not give the talk I had planned. I was used to eager audiences—children who had read my books and were excited to meet the author, or adults who were every bit as interested in books as I am.

My mind raced, trying to come up with a dramatic statement that would get the attention of these boys right away. If I couldn't do that, I knew I might as well save my breath.

The librarian introduced me.

There was no polite applause.

I stood and said, "I once got a brand-new car for writing only twenty-five words."

The eyes opened.

"It was a Honda Civic," I said.

Someone mumbled, "No way," but the boys sat up and listened as I told them about the contests I had won. Then I said I entered the contests because I wanted to be a writer, but nobody bought what I wrote. I explained about the rejections, and how long it had taken me to publish my first book.

Next I talked about some of my books, including *Danger at the Fair*, in which one of the characters steals cars, strips them down, and sells the parts. Heads nodded knowingly. I pointed out that my character ended up in jail.

One of the boys asked how much money I make, so I explained how royalties work. They were indignant when they learned that if someone bought a paperback book for $3.99, I ended up with less than twenty-five cents.

"You should get it all, man," one said.

"I can't paint a picture for the cover," I replied. "I don't know how to print books or bind them together, and since I live in Washington, who would sell my books in Tennessee? I need the publishers and the bookstores and the libraries."

By the time our session ended, we had all learned something.

Three of the boys stayed behind to check out one of my books. The librarian was overjoyed. "Our last speaker left in the middle," she told me, "because the boys were so rude."

I was glad I hadn't known that ahead of time.

Sharing a National Tragedy

Most of my school visits were exciting and fun. Student artwork based on my stories usually decorated the halls; outdoor reader boards said WELCOME PEG KEHRET; every class had read my books aloud; kids jumped with eagerness, impatient to meet the author.

In April 1995, we took the motor home to Oklahoma City to do some school visits. Two nights before we got there, we turned on the television news and learned that the Federal Building in Oklahoma City had been bombed. One hundred sixty-eight people were dead.

Like the rest of the country, we watched in shock as the news unfolded. We drove on to our destination, where I called the librarian or principal of each of the schools that I was going to visit.

"You can cancel if you want to," I told them. "I'll come back another time, if that would be better."

Each of the schools wanted me to come as planned. "We need the distraction," I was told. "We need to think about something besides the bombing."

But how could they? How could any of us?

At the first school, Carl and I were given ribbons to wear in memory of the victims—loops of lavender, yellow, and blue, secured together with a button. Everyone in Oklahoma City wore ribbons, and we wore them, too, every day.

We did not know any of the victims or their families, yet this was a crime against all Americans and we suffered along with those who had lost friends and relatives.

The tragedy overshadowed everything. Children clutched teddy bears in class, seeking comfort from the unthinkable horror.

I talked at a middle school where six students had lost one of their parents and a teacher had lost her brother. The day I was there, a tree was planted on the school grounds as a memorial to the victims.

At another school, I was signing books when a fifth-grade girl hurried in with a book to be auto-graphed. "I'm sorry I missed your talk," she said. "You're my favorite author, but my uncle's funeral was today." I hugged her, and we cried together.

One boy attended a school where I wasn't speak-ing. His mother had him called out of class early so she could bring him to meet me and get some books signed. The boy ran to her car in tears, afraid he'd been excused because another bomb had exploded. He thought his father was dead.

It was not illogical; one of his classmates had been picked up from school early the day of the bombing, to learn he had lost his dad.

Some children lost loved ones; they all lost inno-cence and their sense of security.

The governor of Oklahoma asked for a minute of silence throughout the state, to be observed exactly one week after the bombing. That minute came in the middle of one of my school talks.

The principal had warned me ahead of time that this would happen, but I still was not prepared for the emotion that filled the room. By then we were all beyond tears, yet grief seemed tangible, as if I could reach out and pluck it from the air.

When the minute ended, I couldn't continue to talk about books and writing as if nothing had happened. Instead of my usual remarks, I spoke of my personal belief that the best response when something bad happens is to put some good back into the world. Help someone who needs it. Do a good deed. Be kind.

I talked of my conviction that violence is never a solution, no matter what the problem, and said that this is why the characters in my books use their brains to get out of trouble rather than shooting the villain.

At that time, the bombing of the Federal Building was the worst act of terrorism in our nation's history. My words of comfort felt woefully inadequate, but words were all I had to offer.

We did not visit the site of the bombing that week. Several years later, however, we returned to Oklahoma City and went to the beautiful memorial which is now on the site where the Federal Building once stood.

I will always have a special place in my heart for the people of Oklahoma City. It wasn't easy for those teachers and students to welcome a guest speaker in the midst of their mourning. By celebrating reading and writing together, I hope we put some small good into a time of tragedy.

{ 17 }

Happy Ending

When I was at the Sheltering Arms, I spent two hours every afternoon in the hospital's school. One day the teacher suggested that we each write a letter to our favorite author.

I loved the Betsy-Tacy books by Maud Hart Lovelace, but I refused to write that letter. Mrs. Lovelace was a famous author. I didn't think she'd want to hear from me.

One of my roommates, Dorothy, did write to Maud Hart Lovelace. Two weeks later she got a reply. Not only did Mrs. Lovelace write back, she sent Dorothy a booklet about her life, and the booklet included her photo. I was so jealous I could hardly stand it, but I still never wrote to Mrs. Lovelace myself.

I know now that Mrs. Lovelace would have appreciated a letter from me. I had read all of her books many times, owned three of them, and was in a hospital recovering from polio. No doubt she would have been delighted to learn that her writing gave me pleasure. I'm sorry that I never told her.

I now receive many letters about my books. The best ones are the true fan letters from children who love my books. Many are signed "Your #1 fan" and include a school picture or a list of my books that the child has read. These letters are welcome, and I try to answer them promptly.

Often a class will read one of my books together and then decide to write to me. I'm happy to reply to the class, answering all of their questions.

Letters sent to me in care of one of my publishers are sometimes not forwarded for several months. Far too often, I get mail from kids who are doing an author project on me, but by the time I receive their request for information, school is out for the summer. This problem has eased with the Internet because my mailing address is on my web page (www.pegkehret.com) along with the biographical material that is usually needed.

Sometimes children beg me to write back—but they don't include any return address.

Children frequently ask if I will be their pen pal. I have to say no; I can barely keep up with the correspondence when I answer each person once.

Not all of the mail is from youngsters. Many adults, including me, love children's literature.

A man in Pittsburgh, who learned to read at age forty-six, wrote that *Small Steps* was the first book he ever read. He compared his situation to mine, saying he "is taking small steps to overcome the handicap of not being able to read." He thanked me for encouraging him. Letters like that provide motivation to keep writing.

In 1995, I received the Minnesota Young Reader Award. It is called the Maud Hart Lovelace Award in honor of the Minnesota author whose books I liked so much when I was a child.

I got a letter of congratulations from Miss Beck, my fourth-grade teacher. She enclosed a photograph of Mrs. Lovelace, taken at a library event that Miss Beck had attended in Mankato, Minnesota, decades earlier. Miss Beck said she wanted me to have the picture. What a wonderful gift! I don't have to be jealous of Dorothy any longer.

I am thrilled each time one of my books wins a state "children's choice" or "young reader" award because kids do the voting. Carl had a special necklace made to celebrate these awards. It has a silver charm for each state whose children's book award I've won. The charms are shaped like the states and are engraved on the back with the year and an abbreviation of the winning title.

The necklace is one of my most precious possessions. As of this writing, it has twenty-one charms.

Two other awards are especially meaningful: the 1996 Golden Kite Award in nonfiction from the Society of Children's Book Writers and Illustrators and the 1997 PEN Center West Award in children's literature. Both honors were for *Small Steps*.

If there is ever a Late Bloomer Award, I will surely qualify. I was fifty years old when I published my first book for children.

Once I got started, though, the books flowed from my fingertips to the keyboard nonstop. Perhaps I needed fifty years of living in order to have stories worth telling and to know how to tell them.

As a beginning writer, I listed the three

magazines I most wanted to see my work in. I still set goals, but now they are about the process of achievement rather than the end result. My goals must be something that I can control.

For example, I would love to have movies of my books, but movies are not one of my goals because I can't choose books for the companies that make films. All I can control is how I write the books.

That doesn't mean I can't hope for a movie. Hopes are different than goals.

A movie producer paid for the right to make a movie of *Night of Fear,* and a TV company paid for the right to use the characters in my Frightmares books in a television series, but nothing has happened yet.

So far the closest one of my books has come to being on film was when *Acting Natural* was a prop in a movie made in Canada. An actor talking on the phone picks up a copy of my book and looks at it.

I still hope that a movie will be made of one of my books, but my goals are more practical: Finish five pages a day. Try to make every book entertaining, informative, and insightful. Create characters who solve their problems without resorting to violence. Help readers feel empathy toward all creatures.

Carl and I live in a log house on a ten-acre wildlife sanctuary just twelve miles from Mount Rainier National Park in Washington State. We walk on our nature trail every afternoon and view fabulous sunsets from our porch. My fingers are purple as I type this; earlier today I picked sweet wild blackberries for tonight's dessert.

One room of our house is my office. It has rows of bookshelves, an old library table that I use as a computer desk, and a view of our bird feeders, wildflower meadow, the woods, and far in the distance, on clear days, the Olympic Mountains. Posters of my books hang on the walls, along with a *Time* magazine cover from 1954. The cover picture is of Dr. Jonas Salk, who developed the polio vaccine. The cover is signed by Dr. Salk.

Just as I knew that I would have a happy life whether we adopted children or not, I know that my life today would be joyful, productive, and fulfilled no matter where I lived. Contentment comes from the inside, from the ability to appreciate and savor each day as it unfolds.

Children sometimes ask me, "Are you going to retire?"

I have already quit doing school talks. Because of post-polio syndrome, I tire easily. Book talks at schools take a lot of energy, no matter how much fun they are. I don't speak at out-of-town conferences as often as I used to for the same reason, but being a public speaker was never my job. My job is to write.

I began my career by writing about the neighborhood dogs. I still write about dogs, but now I also write about children who use their wits to resolve their troubles.

I awake each morning ready to work, eager to find out what's going to happen next. As long as readers enjoy my books, I'll continue to write them.

My Ideas Box is overflowing.

by Peg Kehret

Books for Children

I'm Not Who You Think I Am, 1999.

My Brother Made Me Do It, 2000.

Night of Fear, 1994.

Nightmare Mountain, 1989.

Race to Disaster, 1996.

The Richest Kids in Town, 1994.

Saving Lilly, 2001.

Screaming Eagles, 1996.

Searching for Candlestick Park, 1997.

The Secret Journey, 1999.

Shelter Dogs: Amazing Stories of Adopted Strays, 1999.

Sisters, Long Ago, 1990.

Small Steps: The Year I Got Polio, 1996.

The Stranger Next Door, 2002.

Terror at the Zoo, 1992.

The Volcano Disaster, 1998.

The Winner, 1988.

Winning Monologs for Young Actors, 1986

Plays

Bicycles Built for Two, 1985.
Cemeteries Are a Grave Matter, 1975.
Charming Billy, 1984.
Dracula, Darling, 1979.
Let Him Sleep 'Till It's Time for His Funeral, 1976.
Spirit!, 1979.

Books for Adults

Refinishing and Restoring Your Piano, 1985.
Vows of Love and Marriage, 1979.
*Wedding Vows: How to Express Your
Love in Your Own Words*, 1989.